MAGIC INK

ILLUSTRATED BY JIM FIELD

SIMON AND SCHUSTER

A MAGIC INK PRODUCTION

First published in Great Britain in 2013 by Simon and Schuster UK Ltd
A CBS COMPANY.

Design by Jane Buckley

Simon & Schuster UK Ltd
1st Floor, 222 Gray's Inn Road, London WC1X 8HB

www.simonandschuster.co.uk

A CIP catalogue record for this book is available from the British Library.

PB ISBN: 978-1-47114-594-0
eBook ISBN: 978-0-85707-871-1

1 3 5 7 9 10 8 6 4 2

Printed in the UK by CPI Group (UK) Ltd,
Croydon, CR0 4YY

Simon & Schuster Australia, Sydney

Simon & Schuster India, New Delhi

www.magicinkproductions.com

CHAPETR ONE

A MYSTERIOUS PIG IN FANCY DRESS RUNS WILD!

If you noticed I spelled 'chapter' wrong at the top of the page, **CONGRATULATIONS!** I'm just making sure you're awake.

You may think it's a bit crazy to start a book with a wrongly-spelled word. Well, with the story I'm telling, you'd better get used to crazy. And I should warn you, we're talking **bonkers, fruit-loops, round-the-bend, round-the-twist, round-and-round-the-mulberry-bush-then-round-an-extra-twisty-bendy-fruit-loop crazy.** Not throwing the book away in disgust? Good. Then I'll continue. . .

The whole thing started when we saw a pig in a top hat running wild through the house. By "we", I mean my whole family: Mum, Dad and Lib.

Lib – or Liberty – is my little sister. My stupid, whiny, annoying little sister.

She was the first one to see the mysterious pig. . . and to hear it, for that matter.

I was asleep at that point.

Who am I?

Glad you asked.

I'm Stew Penders, and this is my book.

Confession: it's my first go at writing a book and I'm feeling my way a bit. So, please. . . bear with me.

There – a picture! I feel happier when there are drawings involved, you see; I'm more of a comic book kind of guy. I've been writing and illustrating my

own comics since **forever**.

Well, OK, I may have exaggerated slightly there. But from now on, I won't. I don't need to. This true-life story is crazy enough already.

I'll prove it. Let's get back to the night it all began. . .

There was Libs lying in her strange, unfamiliar bed – unfamiliar because we'd only moved into my granddad's old house that very day, and he'd left lots of old furniture behind, and Libs had whined and whined until Mum and Dad shut her up by saying she could have Granddad's big, wooden, sleigh-shaped bed in her room.

Anyway, there she was, surrounded by stuffed animals and princesses and all that rubbish, when suddenly. . .

Snuffle – snuffle —

There's a sinister snuffling outside her bedroom door.

"PIIIIIIIIG!!!" Lib shrieked from across the landing, with way more exclamation marks than I can be bothered to write right now. **"PIIIIIG!** In my BEDROOOOOOM!!! It's got a hat on! Big, fat, hairy **PIIIIIIIIIIIIIIIIIIG!"**

WHAT WAS THAT AT LIBERTY'S DOOR?
WHAT!?
WHAT!?

Luckily for the accuracy of this eyewitness account, that was when I woke up. Nine times out of ten, my automatic response would be to shout something brotherly like, **"LIB, SHUT UP AND STOP BEING SO DUMB!"**

But, on this one-tenth of times, I didn't.

Partly that was because I was in a strange bedroom too, and got confused 'cos I didn't know where I was for a few seconds. But mainly it was because I heard a throaty squeal carry above Lib's cries. And, fair play to her, it did sound *exactly* like the sort of noise a big fat hairy **'PIIIIIG'** might make.

Nah, that's crazy, I told myself. Isn't it?

I checked my watch and saw it was after two in the morning. A split-second later I heard Dad throw open the door to his and Mum's room, which was next door to mine, and shamble outside.

"Something must've got in through the old cat-flap. . ." he said, sounding sleepy and confused. "I don't get it – I boarded the hole up with a piece of two-by-four, a good match for the door, it should've held, no problem. . ."

Dad is a bit of a Do-It-Yourself whizz – or so he likes to think. Eight times out of ten his DIY does it back to him.

But this was no ordinary night.

I was wide awake by now, and waiting for Dad to give Lib a roasting for being stupid, annoying, whiny etc and for making stuff up. But the next moment, *he* was shouting too!

"Bryony!" (That's my mum's name, sorry, should've mentioned that.) "Bryony, there really *is* a pig!"

I almost jumped out of my unfamiliar bed in shock. I heard more squeals and snuffling (by now it was hard to tell whether they were coming from Lib or the pig), quickly followed by a loud *thump* as Dad fell over.

"AAAGH!" he shouted. And then my mum joined in with the caterwauling. Or *pig*erwauling, I guess. Her conversation with Dad went like this:

Mum— "A pig?"

Dad— "Yes, a pig! It got past me, don't come out!"

"But, a PIG?"

"Yes! A pig. Must've got in through the—"

"You mean there's a **PIG IN THE HOUSE?**"

"YES, there's a massive pig up here, it's dressed up in—"

"Did you say **A PIG?**"

"YESSS!"

Their bellowed duet seemed to go on for ages; I can't be sure, because around then I zoned out. Why? Possibly because my unfamiliar bedroom door had suddenly burst open. . . Yellow brightness had flooded in like a strike of lightning. . .

And there was Liberty's pig, poised dramatically in the doorway. Weirdly, I saw that it was wearing a hat – a big, black top hat, like some posh type would wear maybe a hundred years ago. The pig even seemed to have a curly moustache under its snout (a trick of the light, right?!) and its pink, pudgy body was squeezed into a funny kind of coat.

Luckily, I'm not one to panic in the face of strange goings-on and weird events. I'm calm in a crisis, yeah? Stew Penders – the comic book king of cool heads. I stayed smooth and in control and I. . .

Oh, who am I kidding?

I yelled my bum off.

"AAARRRRGHHHHHHHHHHHHH!!!!!!!"

Yep, that was what my scream was like – right down to the bold capital letters and seven exclamation marks.

Well, *you* try meeting a pig in fancy dress in the middle of the night on your first day in a new home! See how you like it!

Besides, I wasn't really scared for myself. All I could think was— *Don't touch my superhero comics! Please! It took me my whole life to collect them and some of them are worth a bit, and bite-marks and trotter-prints are going to* ***seriously*** *reduce their value. . .*

In case you hadn't figured it out, action comics are kind of important to me. What could be more important than super-powered characters in long underwear having fights?

My mum's always despaired of me for being such a comics nut. If I'm not reading about superheroes, I'm drawing my own strips. But, right now, with all of us yelling and shrieking and swearing and falling over, that's exactly what me and my family needed: a superhero. Someone to answer our cries and come bounding to the rescue.

But at that moment, it all boiled down to just two things – a boy in bed, and a pig in top hat and tails with a dodgy 'tache. Each staring at the other.

And then, suddenly, unexpectedly, the pig WINKED. . .

CAPTER THREE

THE PENDERS CONTENDERS

I might just spell a chapter correctly, one day! But don't hold your breath.

There's an old saying that goes something like, 'When heroes don't exist, it is necessary to invent them'. Pretty deep, huh? So, how might my family measure up as superheroes?

Let's weigh up the odds in the big battle – Pig versus Penders – fact-file-style!

THE LIVING TOOLKIT

SECRET IDENTITY:

Nigel Thomas Penders

WHATEVER YOUR PROBLEM, I'LL PUT IT RIGHT! AND PUT UP A SHELF TOO!

KNOWN ALIASES:

Dad, Daddy, Daderoo, Old Man, Lovekins (by my mum).

HOW HE BECAME A SUPERHERO:

While working as an accountant at a nuclear power station, ordinary Nigel Penders was hit on the head by a radioactive toolbox. Soon after, he discovered his body had transformed to take on the powers of different tools at will.

POWERS:

His fists are as hard as hammers. His fingers can turn into super-screwdrivers. His feet can saw through steel. You don't want to know what doubles as a spanner.

CHANCES AGAINST PIG:

50-50 - pigs are notoriously unimpressed by human DIY. . .

ALWAYS-SOMETHING-WRONG-WITH-HER WOMAN

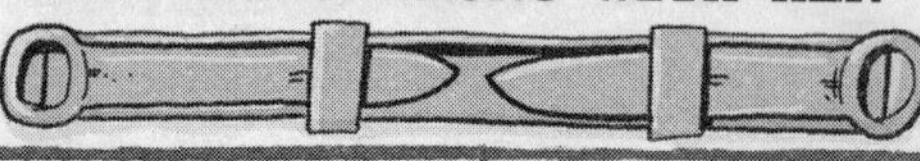

ALWAYS-SOMETHING-WRONG-WITH-HER WOMAN

SECRET IDENTITY:

Bryony May Penders

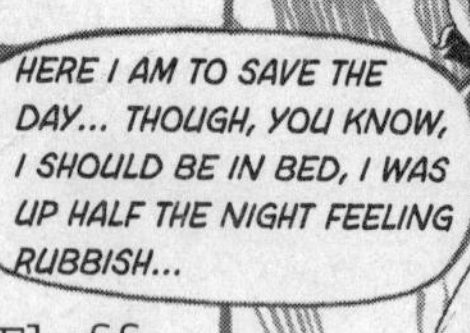

HERE I AM TO SAVE THE DAY... THOUGH, YOU KNOW, I SHOULD BE IN BED, I WAS UP HALF THE NIGHT FEELING RUBBISH...

KNOWN ALIASES:

Mum, Mummy,
Mrs Penders, Honey-Fluff
(by my dad).

HOW SHE BECAME A SUPERHERO:

Bryony Penders was constantly ill with one thing or another. Then, after catching a radioactive germ, she gained the power to infect wrongdoers with a cavalcade of non-life-threatening ailments!

POWERS:

Super-sneeze strong enough to shatter glass, germ-blast from fingers inflicts mild fever, mega-moans about feeling rough all the time can put villains to sleep in seconds.

CHANCES AGAINST PIG:

40-60 - what if the pig retaliates with swine flu?

PAIN-IN-THE-BUTT GIRL

SECRET IDENTITY:

Liberty
Arabella Penders

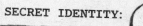

KNOWN ALIASES:

Lib, Libs, Libby, Mummy's Little Angel (by my mum), Daddy's Little Darling (by my dad), Super-Annoying Pest (by anyone else).

EVERYONE LOOK AT ME AREN'T I SPECIAL I'M SECRETLY A PRINCESS AREN'T PONIES SOOOOOO SWEET BLAH BLAH BLAH

HOW SHE BECAME A SUPERHERO:

Born of an alien race, P-I-T-B Girl was dumped on Earth as a baby 'cos she was considered too annoying and whiny. Forever banished from her own planet, she was taken in by Earthling parents who found her 'cute' and somehow she has managed to fool them ever since.

POWERS:

Supersonic irritating whine can inflict massive ear damage. Bores bad guys to death by droning on about ponies, mermaids and other girly rubbish. If attacked by super-villains, she tells their mums and gets them grounded.

CHANCES AGAINST PIG:

Fat zilch.

So, you see, even if they *were* superheroes, three-quarters of my household would be no real use against a killer pig in the middle of the night.

But what about me?

As that bacon-sandwich-in-training stared at me – his top hat cocked at a rakish angle and a glint in his eye – it was almost as if he could see through the outward form of a startled boy to spy the superhero within. The star of a thousand homemade comics, the hero I'd always longed to become. Stew Penders, also known as. . .

STUPENDOUS MAN

SECRET IDENTITY:

Stewart Andrew Penders

KNOWN ALIASES:

Stew, Comics Nerd, Speccy, Super-Geek.

HOW HE BECAME A SUPERHERO:

Ordinary Stew Penders grew up sensing it was no coincidence that his name sounded a bit like 'stupendous'. Then one day he was hit by a radioactive meteorite. It really hurt, so he had to go to hospital, where he was treated for meteorite poisoning. Criminals kidnapped him and performed weird experiments to extract the meteorite's super-powerful properties from his bloodstream. This caused an explosion! Somehow, Stew absorbed its energy, which turned the poison in his veins into pure, pulse-pounding power. Goodbye meteorite, hello meteor-**might** – ***STUPENDOUS MAN*** was born!

POWERS:

HE CAN ABSORB THE PROPERTIES OF ANYTHING HE TOUCHES . . .
HE CAN PASS ON THOSE PROPERTIES TO OTHERS, AND SO DEFEAT HIS FOES. . .
BANK
SWAG
BY TRANSMITTING THESE FRESHLY-ABSORBED WINDOW MOLECULES I CAN TURN YOU TO GLASS!
SMASH!
SM
HE SIMPLY IS. . . STUPENDOUS!

CHANCES AGAINST PIG:

100 per cent triumph over any adversary guaranteed.

Never mind the pig, I hear you shout. Let us read and enjoy Stupendous Man's adventures right away!

Well, I understand where you're coming from. I've been writing and drawing his comic-strip exploits my whole life and right now I'm redrawing and rewriting them (since the earliest ones were a bit basic).

They will be available to read some day. But for now, I'm afraid you HAVE to mind the pig.

In my household, we minded him very much.

After a few seconds' staring at me, the improbable pig suddenly decided to make like the Hulk's trousers – and split. He turned and ran squealing down the stairs, pursued by Dad, with Mum's wails and Lib's screams still ringing in his pink pointy ears.

Within a few minutes, all went quiet. Dad came back and reported that the pig had escaped through what was left of the catflap. The board Dad had used to block it was lying outside on the path to the back door, like it had been prised off. For now, he'd wedged a couple of heavy boxes in front of the hole to keep out any other loopy wildlife.

"A pig in fancy-dress!" Dad attempted a chuckle.

"Most likely a neighbour's idea of a practical joke. You know, we're newbies to the area so they've set us a kind of crazy entrance exam. I'll ask round in the morning – right now we should just forget all about it and go back to sleep."

And so, an uneasy clam settled on the house. Oh, all right then, an uneasy *calm.* But frankly, if there was a mad clothed pig running around there could easily have been an uneasy clam about too.

We wanted to believe there was a normal explanation; and at gone two in the morning, you're ready to believe almost anything.

Libby crashed out eventually after some hugs from Mum and a couple of way-past-bedtime stories from Dad.

It took me longer to drift off, though I was super-tired. I was still awake when the quiet snorts and snufflings started up again. This time from the ceiling.

Or rather, *through* the ceiling.

The noises were coming from the room above mine. The attic. The attic that my granddad had locked up twenty years ago, and banned anyone from going near. . .

I buried my head under the pillow and told myself the noise was in my imagination. I also told myself my carpet was made of marshmallows and that I would one day marry a satsuma.

The three statements were about as believable as each other. But at least the thought of my fruity wedding distracted me long enough to smother my pig-radar and push out some ZZZs in the end.

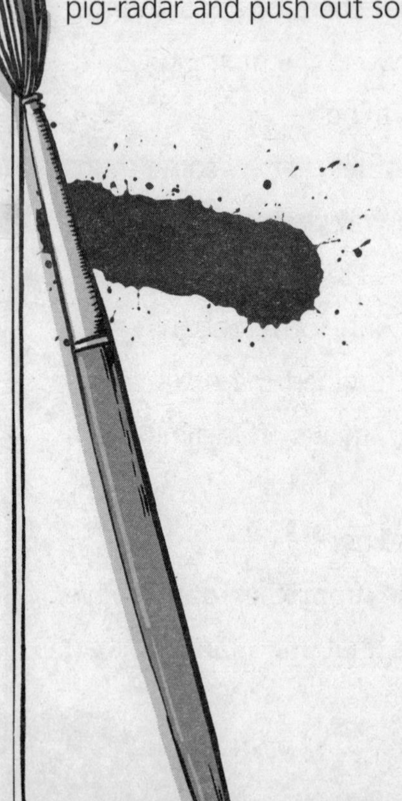

CHAPTER FOR

THE MORNING AFTER

(But you can read it now if you like)

I was woken from a confused dream about marshmallows and small oranges around 8.30 by the sound of banging. It was Dad getting busy with his hammer, nailing a board over the catflap again. He was taking no chances on the pig returning.

I thought about the way the pig had seemed to wink at me. Imagination, I told myself. Got to be. Probably had something in his eye. And the moustache had to be a falsie.

But what about the noises I'd heard in the night? Could there be another animal trapped up there (apart from the uneasy clam, obviously)? Perhaps there was another way in? I couldn't really see a pig climbing a ladder to get in through a hole in the roof. There again, I wouldn't have imagined a pig in a top hat before last night either.

I trudged down the stairs in my dressing gown. I'd been up and down those seventeen steps no end of times before, since I was old enough to crawl, in fact – but to think they were our stairs now and not Granddad's seemed really very odd.

I'd always loved my granddad and couldn't believe he wasn't with us any more. . . that he'd gone to that great comics convention in the sky.

I also couldn't quite believe he had left his savings, his house and everything he owned to his only son – my dad.

On top of that, I also couldn't believe how quickly Dad had stuck our old house up for rent – fully-furnished – so my family could make a new start here on the outskirts of a big town, fifty miles away from our old life in the country (which, by the way, I REALLY LIKED).

But what was *completely* unbelievable was this: instead of using Granddad's money to take us all on a mega-cool vacation, or to buy himself a sports car, or to buy *me* a sports car for when I'm old enough to drive, Dad had chosen to do the most boring, cruel and selfish thing possible:

"Granddad's money will support us while your Mum and I take time out to decide what we want to do with our lives. . ."

You see? Granddad's cash would go on totally boring stuff like supermarket shopping and electricity bills and new shoes, while Dad and Mum skived off from being proper grown-ups.

And it was me and Lib who were paying for their decision: goodbye to our friends, goodbye to our old schools (not exactly heartbreaking, obviously, but still), goodbye to everything we knew. . .

And hello to Granddad's house, to big new scary schools where we knew no one at all – and, apparently, to late-night pig rampages. (And possibly uneasy *clam*-pages.) **[SHUT UP! THERE WAS NO CLAM!]**

It was all right for Lib. She was too small to be that bothered – especially since she got a sleigh bed out of the deal. But for me, it stank.

It stank even worse than the smell coming from the kitchen that morning.

Burning bacon.

Warily, I opened the door. Through a haze of smoke and cardboard boxes I saw Mum snatch a smoking frying pan from the hob with one hand and wrestle a window catch with the other.

Squeezing past the boxes, I helped her to open the window. "Wow." I eyed the burnt-black rashers. "Guess you taught that pig a lesson it'll never forget, huh?"

"I'd certainly like to." The pan hissed angrily on Mum's behalf as she dropped it into the big porcelain sink. "So much for celebrating our first day here with a cooked breakfast. I'm not used to cooking with gas. In any case, I'm a bag of nerves this morning." She jumped as Dad started hammering again in the utility room next door. "See what I mean? There's so much to sort out, and all that banging's giving me the worst headache. . ."

"What a good job it's Easter!" Lib was peeping over the breakfast bar, her saintly smile shining through the smoke. "Me and Stew will be around the whole week to help you."

"Bless you, angel." Mum smiled at Lib fondly.

I smiled at Lib less fondly. "Crawler."

"Nerd." She stuck out her tongue at me. (Six-year-olds – so immature!)

"Don't start," Mum warned us.

Just then, Dad strode out from the utility room and started to choke on all the smoke. "Don't start what?" he gasped.

"Coughing," I said helpfully.

Dad pretended to swing his hammer in my direction, then studied the charred mess in the sink. "Ah. I'm guessing our celebratory cooked breakfast is off the menu?"

"You can have cereal and like it." Mum kicked a cardboard box. "That is, if you can find the stupid cereal anywhere in this mess."

Dad put a caring hand on her shoulder. "There is some good news this morning," he said quietly, opening another window to let out the smoke. "That catflap's closed for good." He waved his hammer cheerily. "I've gone nuclear on it."

"I think I heard something in the attic," I blurted out.

"Last night, after you chased the pig away."

"You did not," Lib retorted automatically.

"What sort of something?" asked Dad.

"A sort of. . . snuffling, scratching sound." I shrugged. "Like an animal."

"Oh, Stew." Mum managed to make the words sound like perfect despair; it was one of her super-abilities. "You and your imagination. There's only the attic above your room, and you know that's been locked up for twenty years."

"Your granddad said we were never to open it, ever," Dad reflected. "But it could be that something's got inside and built a nest or a den up there."

Lib looked worried. "Pigs?"

"Yeah, Lib. Right," I said. "A nest of pigs."

"Pigs could make a den," Lib persisted.

"Nah," I told her, "a den isn't stylish enough for pigs. *Sty*-lish – geddit?"

Lib just sighed, in perfect unison with Mum, who was sorting through the nearest boxes now. "I suppose we'll have to call a pest controller."

"I'll check it out first." Dad looked thoughtful. "I have to admit, I'm dying to know why the old boy locked the attic up – and why he stopped drawing comics at the same time. . ." Now, if *Dad* was dying to know, I was long-since dead and buried with curiosity. That question – Why did Garry Penders suddenly turn his back on comics? – is one of the big, burning mysteries of the strip-cartooning world. There have been all kinds of weird theories. Up till now, no one has ever known the truth.

But they will.

Once they've read this book.

CHAPETR the FIFTH

GARY PENDERS – A LIFE IN COMICS

(And out of comics too, for reasons unknown)

I should warn you up front, the following history-mystery isn't funny. It's serious. Dead serious. Very dead serious. In fact, imagine the deadest thing ever in the world getting shot, blown up, stamped on, squashed by a steamroller, electrocuted and then stuffed into a blender and eaten raw.

That's how dead it is. That's how serious.

Garry Penders – Dad's dad and my granddad – was a **TOTALLY ROCKING COMIC BOOK ARTIST.** He started off illustrating a fanzine about superhero characters. Then he drew a few pages for *Pow* and *Fantastic*, these really old UK comics. He sent the artwork off to comic book firms in the USA, and that got him some work there too.

His stuff went down well. Better than well. The **ACADEMY OF COMIC BOOK ARTS** gave him three awards and he won a ton of other stuff too. But he got kind of fed up, working for all the big companies. He wanted to strike out on his own.

It was around that time that he broke up with my gran and left Dad with her while he travelled the world working on small-time comics in Spain and France and South America – only trouble was, Granddad was so good that the small-time comics didn't stay small-time for long. They became **HUGE, MASSIVE, WHOPPING BIG-TIME COMICS** and made him a fortune. But Granddad never stood still, he kept moving on. . .

Until Gran died, when my dad was twenty-one, and Granddad had to come back to his homeland. A bit like the Mighty Thor returning to Asgard after his exile to Earth.

A bit.

It was around then, maybe two decades ago, that Gary Penders turned his back on superhero comics. Personally, I don't see how anyone could EVER do that. But anyway, a writer he knew had set up a funny comic in this country, *The Belly-Larf!*, kind of like *The Beano*, and for some reason Granddad agreed to work on it.

But he hadn't been doing it for long when SOMETHING happened. No one knows quite what. But whatever it was, it made Granddad stop drawing there and then. He officially retired. Stopped. End of. Finito.

As Stan 'The Man' Lee would say, NUFF SAID.

Told you it was a burning mystery. Thinking about it used to drive me nutty. Until I found out the truth.

Which very nearly drove me completely round the bend and out of sight. . .

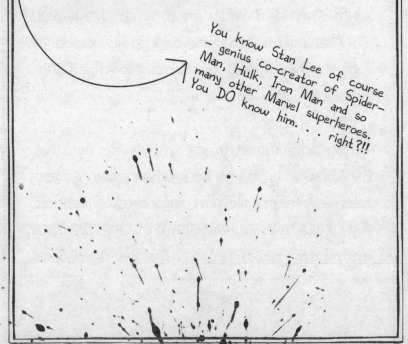

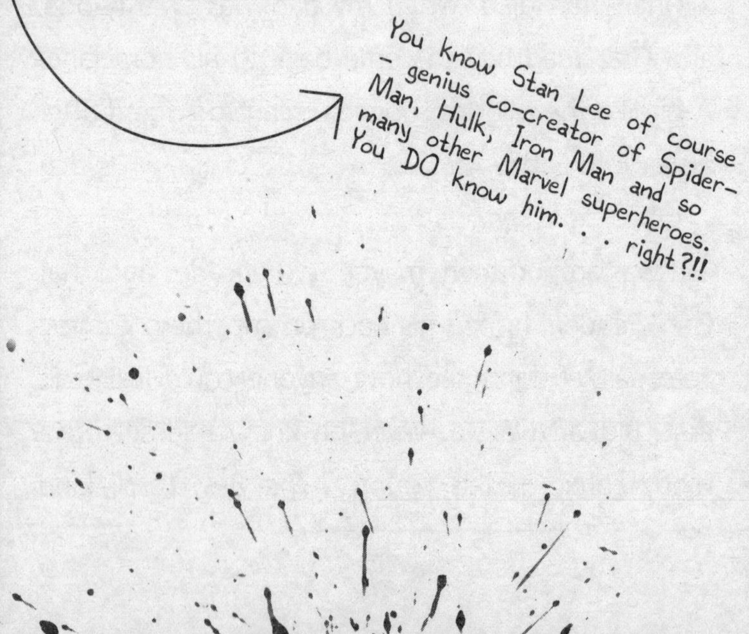

You know Stan Lee of course
– genius co-creator of Spider-
Man, Hulk, Iron Man and so
many other Marvel superheroes.
You DO know him. . . right?!!

CHAP SIX

YEP, WE'RE STILL IN THE KITCHEN

(Can this be possible? Yeah, because it's not so much breakfast as keep breaking-off-to-tell-you-bits-of-back-story-fast. Sorry!)

(And by the way – who IS Chap Six?)

"If Stew thinks he heard noises up in the attic," said Dad, "I definitely think I should take a look."

"Can I come with you?" I gave Dad my most beseeching look. "All Granddad's work will be up there. Please, please, please, please, please—"

"Please, Stew," Mum interrupted. "You already have a room overflowing with silly comics, I don't want you bringing any more down into the house. . ."

"We've got a lot more space here," said Dad tentatively. "It doesn't harm that he takes an interest."

"He should be taking an interest in proper reading!" Mum snapped back.

Obviously, this wasn't the first time Mum had bad-mouthed comic books. As I mentioned a while back, my mother Does Not Approve of comics. Particularly in times of stress. For her, my priceless collection is just a jumble sale waiting to happen.

Weirdly, Dad's never really been a fan of comics either. As a boy he was apparently always the opposite of my granddad, into facts and physics, science and maths, more like Gran and Mum. Sensible, real-life stuff.

No wonder Granddad used to joke, "You're no son of mine!"

And no wonder Mum breathed a little sigh of relief every time she heard him say that. . .

Anyway, the fact of the matter is, Mum is physically incapable of saying the word 'comics' on its own; she always has to qualify it with something sniffy – "ridiculous comics", "awful comics", "dreadful comics", "unpleasant comics". . .

Or – my personal favourite – "*far-fetched* comics".

Of **COURSE** they're far-fetched! They're fetched from about a billion miles away from the normal, boring old world. That's why they're so brilliant. They're fetched from some exotic, epic, exciting land of wonder, action, greatness and lots and lots of skintight lycra.

I always had the feeling that Granddad was kind of pleased I came to have my own major-league lurrrrve for superheroes and all things comic book, since Dad had never really given a radioactive fig-leaf. And yes, Mum was definitely right about one thing – it was **ALL** his fault.

"How come?" I hear you ask. Well, I wound up becoming a comics nerd precisely because my granddad turned his back on comics. He decided to sell off a whole chunk of his super-rare, mega-valuable collection. Today I feel kind of sick to think of him flogging his copy of *Sensation Comics* #1 from January 1942, featuring Wonder Woman's first appearance on a front cover. . . And I **STILL** can't believe that he sold his mint-condition copy of *Amazing Fantasy* #15, with the first appearance of Spider-Man from 1962—

Hey. You'd better not be zoning out right now.

OK, I'll skip some details, but I'm just saying, you could live pretty well for a good few weeks on the kind of cash that each of those comics brought in at auction. And I guess Granddad probably did.

He didn't get shot of everything, though. Seven years ago, when I was a little kid learning how to read, he gave me, like, a couple of tons of old Marvel comic books as a birthday present. Hundreds of them from the 1960s and 70s, decades before I was even born! **The Amazing Spider-Man**s and **Mighty Thor**s and **Daredevil**s and **Incredible Hulk**s and **Conan the Barbarian**s and **Nick Fury, Agent of SHIELD**s and **Captain America**s and **Tomb of Dracula**s and **Marvel Team-Up**s. . . Each one mint or near-mint and bagged and boarded (to keep it in top condition).

To say Mum was not pleased with my instant comic book collection is like saying Doctor Doom was mildly irritated by the Fantastic Four. Because, even though I suddenly had so many comics, I knew – with a wondrous, pulse-pounding certainty – that **I HAD TO HAVE MORE.**

And so, through the past, I got into the present. I got Blu-Rays or DVDs or downloads of all the Marvel movies that have come out (*Spider-Man 2*! Is there any film in the world better than *Spider-Man 2*?

Well, maybe *Marvel Avengers Assemble*). I trawled car boot sales for cheap Marvel videogames, and ransacked the web for fan sites and Wiki guides to learn what I'd missed. My weekly allowance went exclusively on grabbing mail-order back copies of my fave titles. . .

ANYWAY. . . I guess the real story I'm here to tell you began properly later that morning.

In the next chapter.

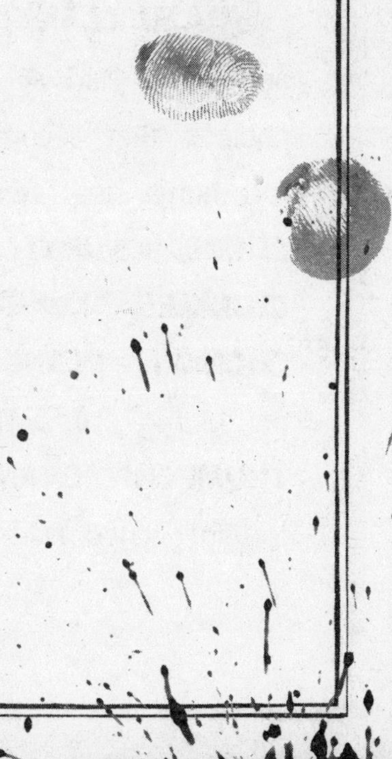

CHAPETR SEVEN

ARCTIC EXPLORERS

(Well, 'ATTIC' explorers really. But 'Arctic' sounds cooler. Extremely cold, in fact. Whereas the attic was fairly warm.)

After the Bacon Sandwich That Never Was and the Cereal That Couldn't Be Found (meaning we all ended up with burnt toast moistened with butter and Mum's despairing tears), Dad decided that right now was the perfect time for him to force open that long-ago locked attic door. . .

WHAM! CLANK! Ka-CRUNCH! With hammer and chisel Dad set about the heavy chain and padlock that secured the attic door handle to the huge steel hooks in the wall either side. **CLINK! KWUNK! CHANK! CLONK! BAMP! CLUNKLE! Ker-PLING! WHOMP! BANG! CHONKK! PLANG! KLUNNG!** (Yes, he kept on hitting it.) **SMANK! BWUMP! KLONG! THUMPCH! CRANG! SCLUNCH!** ("Oww! My thumb!" cried Dad, trying not to swear in front of me. "Owww! Arrrgh!") **PANG-PRANG-PRING-PLUNG! CRUNNG! KLANNGLE!**

Sorry, but it took him a long time. . .

Finally – **Pa-KLANKK!** – the chain gave way and – **TOMP!** – the padlock fell to the floorboards. The attic door was freed.

Dad and I gazed at it in uneasy wonder. Then we shared a Significant Look. We knew that this was a big deal for us both in different ways; suddenly we had access to a part of Granddad's life on which he had literally closed the door, never to be spoken of again.

I felt sad for a few moments and wished Granddad was still here, with us. Except, of course, he'd be shouting and yelling and going mental at us for breaking into his attic – so maybe it was better that Dad and me were doing this alone.

I'd asked Granddad so often if I could see inside that attic where he used to work, and every time his eyes would kind of cloud over and his lips would press tight into a sharp little line and he'd shake his head and go quiet, and that was the end of the conversation.

Now, finally, we were about to learn the reason why. . .

Dad led the way inside the gloomy, musty room. He tried the light switch – nothing doing – but my wide eyes could see well enough. The room was long and thin with exposed beams. The curtains were half-open, and there was a skylight in the sloping roof, but the glass was caked with decades' worth of dirt and let little light through.

I saw Granddad's drawing board, just as he must've left it – well, aside from a coating of dust – and a rickety, ink-stained stool beside it. A comfy armchair sat at the far end of the room behind a coffee table scattered with papers and magazines.

But my attention was seized by the framed pieces of comic book art hanging on the wall – originals, by the look of them. Some had been drawn by Granddad, others by amazing artists like Jack Kirby and Steve Ditko. (Never heard of them? Go and look them up!) There were certificates and honours and awards on the mantelpiece and photos of Granddad looking way younger and lots happier than I'd ever seen him.

As I gazed around, my eyes must've been out on stalks, because Dad looked over and gave me a little smile. "No obvious signs that anything's got in here," he said. "The windows are closed and I can't see any droppings. . ."

I suddenly took in the yellowed paper taped to Granddad's desk. On it was a cartoonish figure picked out in lines of deep, easy-flowing indigo. . .

A figure that held me transfixed.

A figure that sent my heart heaving up into my throat, that unlatched my jaw and dropped it open, that whumped me in the tum and left me boggling, that took my butt-cheeks and made them tremble—

All right, all right. I'll get on with it.

It was the figure of a cheeky-looking, moustachioed pig in a top hat and cape. Winking.

Hmm. Where-oh-where had I seen that figure before?

Oh, yeah, that's right: **RUNNING AROUND MY HOUSE LAST NIGHT, SCARING EVERYONE TO DEATH – AND WINKING AT ME.**

"Aha!" Dad cried, and I jumped like I'd just taken

20,000 volts. "Look here, Stew." He'd picked up some comics from the coffee table. "Last night's fun and games was definitely linked to your old granddad. Here's the proof."

No, **HERE'S** the proof, I was about to say, pointing to the drawing board. But as Dad crossed to join me he held out an old copy of *The Belly-Larf!* – that humour title Granddad had taken on to help out a friend. It wasn't a comic I knew well, and right now I didn't want to know it at all. Because there, pride of place on the front cover, was an all-too familiar winking, top-hatted, curly-tailed character. . .

LARFS WITH POSHO PIG! screamed the cover line. **See page 7!** "He's got the same pig on his drawing board too. . ." Recognising Granddad's style at once, I turned to page seven of the comic. There was a well-drawn, nine-frame strip about a cheeky, upper-crust pig having a noisy party on his farm and outwitting his posh human neighbours when they tried to complain. "Posho 'swill' be here again for more fun and pranks next issue," promised a line at the bottom of the page.

LARFS with POSHO PIG!

SEE PAGE 7!

"He probably drew that pig's cartoon every week," said Dad, checking through some of the other mint-condition *Belly-Larfs!.* "You know, I do vaguely remember Posho, now I've seen this again. I'll bet a neighbour always liked that strip, and that's why they dressed up the pig last night in the same way – for a practical joke, as I said." He put down the comics on the drawing board. "Or maybe the pig got loose without its owner knowing. Tests have shown that pigs are the sixth cleverest animal in the world."

"Cleverer than the guy who thought intelligence tests for pigs were worth bothering with, anyway," I said, looking back at the drawing board and studying the Posho there with a critical eye. The paper was weird, discoloured. More like parchment.

There was a brush on the built-in shelf beneath the drawing board, its fine head stained dark; Granddad must've used it to ink the Posho pic. Reverently, I picked up the brush – and frowned.

The brush had been left covered in Indian ink, so the bristles should've been crusty and stiff. But instead they were soft and fine, good to go, as if the brush had been used twenty seconds ago, not twenty years. I pinched the bristles between the finger and thumb of my left hand. Both finger and thumb came away stained with ink. How come?

"Hey, Stew!" Dad's voice jarred me from my thoughts. "Did you ever see anything like these comics? They must be seriously old. . ."

He came over with a pile of paper the colour of old wee in a toilet that someone had forgotten to flush. Like the stuff on the drawing-board, it was stiff and rough. The cover showed an impressive-looking knight swinging a huge, shining sword, with a kind of logo above it in a weird-looking language: DUX BELLORUM, it read.

The pages were folded over in the middle like a comic book except they were bound together with a thin purple ribbon rather than staples. And each page was busy with heroic knights grappling with unknown warriors, all inked in that same rich, dark purple-blue.

"It's like a comic from a thousand years ago." I peered at the ornate script in the speech balloons;

it looked like the sort of thing an old monk from the Middle Ages would come up with. "What language is that?"

COMEDE MEUM FUSTUM, STULTISSIME! VAE MATREM TUAM - QUAE TAMQUAM PISCIS VETERRIMUS ODORATA EST!

"Maybe Latin?" Dad flicked through another of the comics, then smiled. "But this bit's in English." He pointed to a small box on the cover.

MAGIC, INC.

"MAGIC, INC.?" I breathed.

"As in, 'incorporated'," Dad explained. "It must be the name

of the company who published it. P'raps Granddad put these strips together for Magic, Inc. as a marketing gimmick? You know, for a comic about knights."

"The art in these things isn't Granddad's," I told him. "It's a completely different style."

Dad shrugged and leafed through another of the stiff, yellowed bundles. "If you say so."

After a while you come to recognise an artist's style – you know, from the way he presents and frames his characters. And the characters in this strip were all knights and kings and stuff; they looked powerful and dynamic, perfectly proportioned, with a real sense of movement from panel to panel. As the characters fought, their battle built up like a storm, growing more intense and energetic with every turn of the yellowed paper until finally, in a full-page splash of double-fab drama, the king-dude smashed the last armoured warrior with a killer right-hook, right off the edge of a cliff.

I looked again at the cover and felt a shiver crawl snail-slow down my backbone. Where had these old comics come from? How could ink so old stay wet all this time? What had gone on here twenty years ago to make Granddad shut this room off from the rest of the house. . .?

And was it over?

I was just about to show Dad the ink smeared on my fingers when suddenly—

"OINK!"

Dad's bundle of parchment comics exploded in all directions as he jumped, and I yelled out too, whirling round in shock – to find the attic door had been shoved open as a small, hideous figure burst inside. . .

CHAPTE'IGHT

BACK TO THE DRAWING BOARD

(LITERALLY)

It was my little sister, Lib – and she was laughing her head off. "Got you!" she giggled. "Made you jump!"

Dad humoured her with a smile.

I didn't.

"I'll make you jump!" I roared. **"Right down the toilet!"** And I chased Lib out of the attic. She squealed and hared back down the stairs towards her bedroom. Just as I was about to catch her on the landing, Mum stepped out of her room with a pile of boxes and got between us. Lib, being small, ducked down and made it past. Me, being bigger, went **THUMPCH!** straight into Mum before I could stop and we both went down in a hail of boxes.

Well, you can imagine the ruckus.

I had to keep a low profile for the rest of that day.

Sulking on my bed, mainly. It was less effort than starting to unpack the boxes piled up all around me. To take things out of those boxes was to accept that I would be staying here in Granddad's strange old house, and I wasn't quite up to facing that.

The stain on my fingers refused to wash out. However much I scrubbed at it, however much liquid soap I squooged onto it, however hard I tried, it just wouldn't shift. I wouldn't normally have minded, but later that night, after lights out, as I carefully unwrapped and pulled out issue 143 of The Mighty Thor, I somehow left behind an indigo smear on the front cover, ruining the comic completely – or downgrading it from Near Mint to Good condition at the very least.

What was up with this ink? It hadn't rubbed off on anything else. How could it still be wet after all this time?

Then – **DING!** An idea.

If I could find the ink bottle, maybe there would be washing instructions on the label or something. I figured it was worth a shot.

So I took my torch and crept upstairs. I didn't want to get in any more trouble. If I got ink smudges all over the duvet or the wallpaper or something, Mum would explode (making even more mess).

The house was silent. The night was cloudy. The stairs were creaky. The landing was cold.

The door to the attic stood ajar.

I flitted inside like a ninja shadow and trained my torch on the drawing board. If the brush had been left there, surely the bottle would be somewhere close by. . .

"Is this what you're looking for?" came a low, well-spoken voice.

I swear my heart turned into a snowball. My breath caught in my throat and I felt I might puke with fear.

As I swung the torchbeam towards the voice, my legs turned to mush. Otherwise I would've run downstairs yelling and shouting for my mum and dad, before hiding under the bed and staying there for approximately forever.

Because there, in my torchlight, was the pig. The pig with the face-fuzz, the cape and the top hat.

Only this time he was standing on his hind legs and holding something in one trotter.

A bottle of ink.

I stared in dread and wonder at the apparition before me. **"P-P-P-Posho Pig?"**

"In the living pork-and-bacon flesh," said Posho Pig. **"Oink!"**

This must be a dream, I thought. Yeah. It's bound to be a dream.

Obviously, it wasn't.

"Oink!" the intruder went on. "My dear chap, you won't believe how long we've been waiting for you."

I gulped. "We? Who's we?"

"The Big Man and I. But, first things first, Stewart Penders." The impossible pig smiled. "You and I have a lot to talk about. An awful lot. **Oink!** Emphasis on the awful, I'm afraid."

With a snort and a snuffle, Posho walked slowly towards me. . .

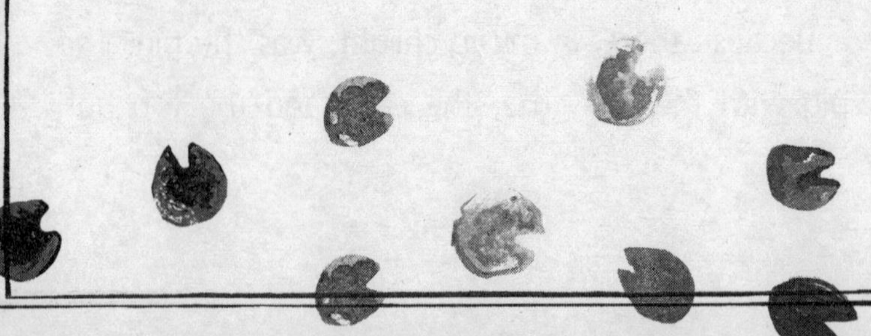

CHAPTER NIN-E

SPOOKY FATEFUL STUFF

(WITH ADDED PIG)

Looking back, I guess you could say it was a moment of destiny. Know what I mean? One of those rare, fantastic times when you don't react in the way you ought to – you know, dribbling, screaming and generally losing your mind – because on some cosmic level you understand what's happening. Some inner purpose you never knew about is soon to be realised. . . and it always had to be this way.

(This kind of thing happens in Superhero Land a lot. The ordinary and the exotic crash together time after time, and lives are changed FOREVER.)

"That ink stain on your fingers," said Posho, pausing in his advance, "proves that you are marked out for greatness."

It's not every night a pig tells you something like that.

"Greatness?" I whispered. "Me?"

"You, old chum," Posho agreed, putting down the inkpot with one of his trademark winks. "**Oink!** Would I tell you porky pies?"

It was so strange – in the light of my torch Posho might have been a real pig standing on his hind legs. Yet there was something more than ordinarily piggy about him – it was as if a larger-than-life animatronic character had just jumped out from some crazy movie. He held himself with confident control. The clothes he wore fitted perfectly – just as in the comic strip. His lips moved improbably when he talked, wiggling his moustache as they did so. And his voice sounded sort of upper class, very human.

Something told me that this particular pig would come way higher than sixth in one of those weird animal smartness tests. . .

Feeling extremely un-smart, I couldn't think of anything to say. So I just stood there, staring.

And what happened next was like something straight out of the pages of *The Belly-Larf!*. . .

"Of course, some stains do not mark you out for greatness," Posho went on. "Like, the stain of strawberry sauce."

From nowhere, a squirty bottle appeared in Posho's trotters – and a jet of red goo splattered all over Stew. "Ugh!"

"The stain of a custard pie is even worse!" Posho continued, hurling a big foamy flan at Stew's face.

Stew didn't duck in time and wound up with most of it on his head. "Stop it!" he spluttered.

"My dear chap, I was made this way..." Posho produced a bucket of soapy water. "I'm the porky king of japes."

"How can you be real?" Stew grabbed the bucket of water before he was made to wear it. "Where did you come from?"

"Am I going crazy?" I added. But as I wrestled Posho for the bucket, I was close enough to brush against his warm, bristly skin, to feel the hot little breaths puff from his snout, to smell his not-really-very-pleasant piggy perfume. And, all at once, it hit home hard enough to hurt:

"You're really real," I murmured.

"Yes," sighed Posho. "Real enough to feel rather lonesome after two decades locked up by myself. **Oink!** I mean, it's hard to be a clever, joke-playing pig when you've got no one to trick or talk to." He gave me a lofty look. "And when finally you do meet someone, all they can do is babble at you. **Oink! Oink!** Well, I suppose we should get the explanations out of the way."

"Yes," I said. "I think so."

Posho sat down on Granddad's stool. It was kind of weird to see a pig sit like a person. But things were about to get weirder.

"Simply told, your grandfather created me, old chap," said Posho. "One night he drew me with magic ink on this very special piece of parchment you see on his drawing board, and—" he jabbed a trotter up at the skylight – "**Oink!** When moonlight touched that illustrious illustration, I sprang to majestic, pig-tastic life!"

"Whoa, whoa, rewind," I said. "Magic ink? Special piece of parchment?"

"**Oink!** Yes, yes, the ink, a particular piece of blank parchment to write on, the ancient comics – they were all buried in the garden out there, centuries ago so that one day your grandfather would find them."

I stared at Posho, incredulous. "How?"

"By digging them up with a spade, I suppose."

"No, I mean, who could possibly have known back then that Granddad would end up living here?"

"It was foretold." Posho smiled. "Anyway, you asked me what I was doing in the house last night. **Oink!** I'm terribly sorry, I only came downstairs to get this bucket and some pie ingredients and that strawberry sauce. You see, I've never been able to play my pranks properly before. . ."

Suddenly I saw a box of rice crispies lying overturned behind him. "*That's* where the cereal went! Mum almost had a breakdown looking for that packet!"

"I put them in the pie-mix. Economy brand, that's all they're good for – my dear boy, how do you cope?" Posho shook his head disapprovingly. "**Oink!** Anyway! You can't blame me for wanting to check on who'd moved in. I'm used to having the run of the place – I come and go as I please, in and out through the window there and up and down the ivy."

"A pig who climbs walls. . . " My head was starting to spin.

Perhaps Posho noticed my pained expression. "It's all right, old bean," he said gently, "you're not the only one who finds recent developments hard to believe. I've been waiting for twenty years for your granddad to unlock that attic door and come inside and do what he was supposed to." The pig hung his head. "Now he's dead and gone. My creator, no more! And did anyone think to invite me to the funeral? No! They didn't even ask me to go along to the buffet afterwards. Outrageous rudeness. . . !"

Posho was getting himself in a state. I wondered if my parents might hear and come upstairs, and realised I didn't want them to. Whatever madness was going on up here in the attic, I somehow knew it was *important* madness.

"No one even knew you were up here," I broke in quickly. "So how could they invite you?"

Posho stared at me. "Hmm. . . I suppose you may have a point." He fiddled with his top hat. "But you can't blame me for being sensitive. My creator ran off as soon as he clapped eyes on me and locked me away so I couldn't complete my task. That wasn't supposed to happen."

"What task?" I hissed, trying to stay patient. "What was supposed to happen? And what's it got to do with me and this ink-stain?"

Posho looked me straight in the eye. "Your grandfather turned chicken, old boy. You must not. I can provide help and support, but it's **YOU** the Big Man will have to rely on in the struggles ahead, Stewart – a descendant of the chosen one. Someone who believes in heroes, someone who has the drive and the passion to create characters who are larger than life. . . because the Big Man's life is at stake."

I was boggling so hard I thought my brain might blow a fuse. "What do I have to do? Who is the Big Man?"

"**Oink!** Why, the same fellow who made the magic ink and buried it back in the 6th Century," said Posho. "Merlin!"

I paused. "Merlin? Merlin. . . as in, Merlin?"

"**Oink!** Yes, as in, Merlin, the wizard Merlin."

"The wizard. . . Merlin. King Arthur's mate?"

"That's him. Most famous wizard ever."

". . . Merlin?"

"Yes! **Oink!** How many more times!"

I didn't know the answer to that question. I must've looked like a goldfish, opening and closing my mouth. And I felt like one too, suddenly unable to hold a thought in my head for more than a second. Finally, I was jolted back to normal by the creak of a door opening downstairs. I heard Dad come out onto the landing, and call, in his hoarse whisper, "Stew? Are you up there?"

Posho and I stared at each other in agonised silence. Then the mystery pig waved, scampered to the window, lifted the latch soundlessly and dived outside. A stealthy rustle of ivy was my only clue that he was climbing down out of sight.

Like a boy in a dream I switched off the torch, walked from the attic and pulled the door shut behind me. I heard Dad call again, quietly, "Stew? Come down!"

"Sorry, Dad," I whispered, padding down the steps. "I. . . thought I heard something in the attic again. But nothing was there."

"Of course it wasn't." Dad tried to be gruff, but I could tell he was relieved. "Now, just stay in bed, OK? If you think you hear anything, come to me. Your mum and I thought we had burglars for a minute there."

Not burglars, I thought. A talking pig. Who knows Merlin!

Suddenly I understood why Granddad had locked up the attic and never gone back. And now, too late, I wished that Dad had never broken inside, that I had never touched that stupid brush, that I had. . .

But, as all us superheroes know, you can't fight fate.

I jumped at a tapping on my bedroom window. There was Posho Pig clinging on outside, waving and giving me a big trottery thumbs-up.

I had the sinking feeling that whatever Granddad had begun, I would be expected to finish.

BUT. . .

What if it finished me first?

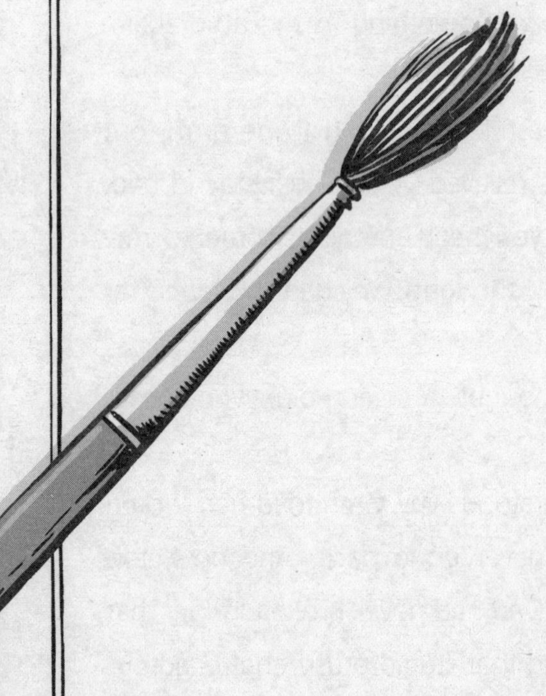

CHAPTA TEN

WILL THE REAL MERLIN PLEASE STAND UP

(OR LEVITATE OR DO A COOL TRICK OR SOMETHING?)

When I woke up the next morning, I did my best to pretend nothing had happened.

It worked really well for at least two-and-a-half seconds.

By then I'd risked a peek at my thumb and seen the ink stain was still there. A queasy feeling built up quickly in my stomach – a seasick mixture of night-before-Christmas excitement and eve-of-an-exam panic.

Magic, I thought. It's real.

Yeah. Real freaky.

And it felt like it was wiping its real magicky, freaky butt all over me.

"Stew, breakfast!" Mum called, making me jump.

I opened my bedroom door warily and stepped outside.

"I hope she's not planning to give you more of that rotten economy cereal," came a familiar voice from the top of the stairs.

I jumped at the sight of Posho, bright-eyed and peering down at me from under the brim of his top hat. But this time I only jumped about two metres into the air, not three.

Yeah, I was getting used to weirdness.

"Oink!" Posho went on. "We need to finish our little talk, old chap. Don't you think?"

"Is this really all about Merlin?" I asked suddenly.

Posho smiled a little sadly and nodded.

"But, he must've been alive. . . like, thousands of years ago."

"Don't be ridiculous!" Posho chuckled. "**Oink!** It was only one-and-a-half thousand years ago."

I swallowed hard. Well, the pig's story was kind of hard to swallow, you must admit.

"Uh, OK," I said. "I'll be back later."

And I ran downstairs.

As I came into the kitchen it felt like the most normal place in the world. So normal, it felt almost suspicious. Lib was slurping cereal with a pink furry unicorn on her lap, Mum was looking tired beside the toaster, Dad was letting his tea cool as he read the newspaper. . . It was like everyone had been taking normal lessons from Mr Norman Normal of Normal Street, Normalville in the United States of Normality.

And suddenly I felt like such a freak. Like I didn't belong here in this normal world. Not with a magic pig waiting for me upstairs.

But then a possibility occurred to me. Maybe Posho the prankster pig was putting me on – or simply mistaken? Maybe the Big Man was just someone *calling* himself Merlin. That would mean Posho had been brought to life with ink from just some random scary magical person instead of the original scary magical person.

Hooray!

Yeah, big whoop.

But exactly who was this original scary magical person? In case it really *was* Merlin, I needed to know more. . .

That afternoon, I found Dad setting up his computer downstairs. Mum had spent most of the morning on the phone trying to get our Internet connection sorted out and – inevitably – had given herself a headache. So I kindly offered to test our online status straight away. . .

By typing 'Merlin' into the search engine.

There was lots of stuff about the wizard on TV and in films. But what about the real Merlin?

Guess what – there didn't seem to be one!

All the websites agreed that Merlin never really existed. It seemed that his character was partly based on some Welsh loony from the 4th Century who ran around naked while predicting the future, and partly based on some old royal soldier type.

Neither of these guys was anything to do with King Arthur. It wasn't until the Middle Ages that the two were put together, and Merlin was rebooted and reinvented for new stories for new audiences. . .

Holy tights and long underwear, I thought with a tingling thrill of excitement. That makes him just like a comic book character!

Take Spider-Man, for instance. There's the regular mainstream Spidey, but there's also *Spider-Man Marvel Adventures*, *Spider-Man: Chapter One*, the old Spider-Man movies, the latest Spider-Man movies, loads of Spidey cartoons. . . All different takes on the same hero.

I guess maybe Merlin was a similar thing, one of the first superheroes of his day. Different people had different ideas of who he was and what he did, changing the details to appeal to different audiences. And suddenly one day he was this wise old guy who protected King Arthur and cast spells and advised him and foretold the future. . .

I pieced together what I'd learned about Merlin from the famous old stories:

MERLIN WAS BORN. HIS DAD WAS A DEMON.

HE WAS A BIT OF A SHOW-OFF, CHANGING HIS SHAPE TO IMPRESS PEASANTS.
PRETTY COOL, HUH, LADIES?
UGH!
WHEN KING ARTHUR'S DAD BUILT A TOWER THAT KEPT FALLING DOWN, MERLIN WORKED OUT THE TROUBLE. THERE WERE TWO DRAGONS FIGHTING UNDERNEATH.
IT'S EITHER DRY ROT OR DRAGONS. I'M THINKING MAYBE DRAGONS.
IN TIME, MERLIN BECAME KING ARTHUR'S WIZARDLY ADVISOR. . .
FINISH IT WITH WHITE STONE, ARTHUR - IT'LL LOOK MAGIC!
. . . AND FELL IN LOVE WITH A MEAN HUNTRESS CALLED VIVIANE.

BAH!
BYEEEEEE!
VIVIANE WASTED NO TIME IN TURNING MERLIN'S MAGIC AGAINST HIM, TRAPPING HIM FOREVER IN A CAVE.

That was as much as I could work out from all the conflicting accounts, as Merlin's franchise was rebooted time and time again. How much of it would be true? None of it, surely. . .

Or **ALL** of it?

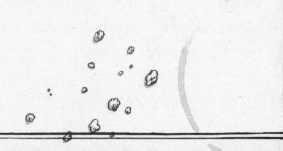

CHAPT'ELEVEN

INKY REVELATIONS

With a head stuffed full of Arthurian legends, I mooched upstairs to my room and shut the door, troubled. Real or otherwise, why (and how) the hecking flip would Merlin have come to my granddad for help, centuries and centuries ahead in his future?

With a tingling sensation of doom, I looked down, and saw my blighted copy of Thor #143 still lying on the floor.

With a jolt I found I could no longer read the words at the bottom of the cover where the ink had smudged. Somehow, bizarrely, where it used to proclaim: 'Balder the Brave! The Stunning Sif! This is IT!', it now said: 'Blah-de-blah-blah' in the same unreadable old-style writing as on those Magic, Inc. comics in the attic.

And, suddenly, I had one of those lightbulb-over-the-head moments. An idea!

This idea of mine that seemed clever but proved not to be in the long term (as you will find out) was to try wiping my weird inky fingers on the words in the old parchment comics upstairs. After all, if the ink turned normal words into gibberish, maybe they'd turn gibberish into normal words.

In a world that no longer made sense, it seemed the only sensible thing to try. So, with my heart scampering about my chest like a deranged hamster, I crept upstairs. . .

The attic was empty. It seemed a little brighter than it had before. I saw the bucket of soapy water that Posho had almost hurled over me now stood empty, and I realised that the skylight had been washed clean, transformed into a rectangle of pale evening sky. There was no sign of the pig but I saw the old comics were stacked in a neat pile on the coffee table.

I picked up the yellow parchment in my right hand and wiped my dirty finger over the title of DUX BELLORUM.

Like magic, the words reformed to spell: WAR COMMANDER.

I almost dropped the comic book. The power of this stuff – it was scary.

Freaked out and yet encouraged at the same time, I turned to the panel I'd been admiring before (on p.42, remember?) and smeared my thumb over the words. In a blur, I could read them! With shivers

EAT MY MACE, DOLT! WOE BE TO THY MOTHER, WHO SMELLS LIKE AN OLD FISH!

shimmying along my spine, I turned my attention (and thumb) to the splash page. That's the big, cool image you normally get at the front of a comic, designed to entice you in – in this case, a knight galloping along on horseback.

Breath held, I wiped my indigo stain over the caption boxes at the bottom of the page. They turned out to be the credits, showing the team responsible for that particular comic book.

And as the letters merged and melted, the talent behind War Commander was revealed. . .

Script by MERLIN. Drawn by MERLIN. Inked by MERLIN. Lettered by MERLIN. A Magic, Inc. Production (Magic, Inc. owned by MERLIN)

I stared down at the paper, shaking my head, chills rifling through my bones. "The great wizard Merlin," I murmured. "Sorcerer, magician, advisor to King Arthur and. . . frustrated comic book artist?"

"**Oink!** That's exactly right, old bean." Posho had suddenly appeared, his eyes bright and his topper askew; I guess he'd crept in through the window. "And tonight, when the moon is full and the shadows long. . . " He held up a piece of parchment with nine neat blank boxes arranged in three rows. "You, Stew, will soon be drawn into a conversation with the mystical Merlin. . . **Oink!** You will make comic-strip contact with the Big Man himself!"

CHAPETR TWELVE

GETTING READY FOR MY UNCANNY STRIP COMMUNICATION WITH THE ONE AND ONLY MERLIN

I'm going to cut to the chase, now. Which means skipping the normal stuff that happened that day like tea with my family (takeaway pizza), watching TV (nothing good on) and trying (but failing) to read a book (I can't remember what it was but obviously it was nowhere near as good as this one).

I wanted to text my best mates back home but didn't know what to say; we were far enough apart as it was, and if they thought I'd gone completely crazy since moving they might stop talking to me all together.

Anyway, picture me sitting in Granddad's attic, later that night. While Dad, Mum and Lib were counting sheep (or, more likely, counting power-tools, headache pills and mermaids riding unicorns, respectively), I was feeling stupendously scared.

Here I was facing up to whatever Granddad had turned his back on. Why? Why didn't I just tell my parents, or run away from home, or. . .

"YOO-HOOOOO. STEW! COO-EEEEEEEEEEE!"

You hear that? Destiny was calling.

The climb up the attic stairs seemed to last hours. A curious shine came from inside the room – it was the silvery moonlight beaming through the skylight. It fell onto the old drawing board; Posho stood beside it like a bacon-scented sentry, a smile on his face. I saw that the parchment page with its nine panels was already taped in place.

"Good chap. I knew you'd go through with it," Posho murmured. He raised the old pot of ink in one trotter and the inking brush in the other.

I took the inking brush doubtfully. "I. . . I normally use a felt-tip."

"It's the magic ink that will let you speak to Merlin across the centuries." Posho nodded solemnly. "**Oink!** An ordinary felt-tip will be no good at all."

"Across the centuries?" I echoed. "You mean, he can speak to me. . . from the past?"

"He is trapped there," said Posho grimly. "Don't worry. The Big Man will explain."

"OK, but. . . " I stared at the empty comic strip panels. "What am I supposed to draw, in any case?"

"Why, Stewart Penders, of course, old chap." Posho smiled. "**Oink!** It's a conversation, isn't it? So, to focus the connection over the ink-link, you draw a picture of yourself, and you write your questions and answers—"

"In a speech balloon?" I hazarded.

"Go to the top of the class." Posho smiled piggily. "Merlin will respond in kind with his own illustrations."

I felt seriously doubtful about it all. But then, Dad did have a game app on his phone where a bunch of players around the world hook up and take it in turns to draw pictures and guess what they're meant to be. I suppose this was kind of the same – just a whole lot weirder and creepier.

"Hang on, though," I said, "won't the moonlight bring my drawing to life?"

"This is talking paper," said Posho. "Talking paper is quite different to the living paper from which

I sprung. **Oink!** It's been charmed in an entirely different way to allow you to communicate. I do wish you'd pay attention!"

"Well, pardon me. . . !" I walked over to the drawing board. "I wonder where Granddad kept his dip pen? It's, like, an old-fashioned pen you use with ink. I prefer it to a brush."

"**Oink!** You'll find two in the tin on the shelf over there."

I opened the tin reverently, ditched the brush and picked out the precious dip pen – a Hunt Hawk Quill 107, to be precise. What characters had Granddad drawn with it? I wondered. To think I was holding it just as he would've held it as he perfected page after page of comic book cool. . .

This was awesome. Beyond awesome.

My jitters left me. I dipped the nib into the magic ink—

And began to draw.

It was kind of tricky, using the dip pen. I tried to pretend Granddad was watching and giving me tips, like he used to. You can't press too hard or you'll

damage the nib, he'd say. And you have to keep your arm moving so the ink flows smoothly…

Well, my efforts weren't too smooth, but I managed to put an OK self-portrait in the panel.

Now it was time for the lettering. . .

"What should I say?" I wondered aloud.

"Greet the big man," Posho suggested. "**Oink!** Say it is your honour to serve him."

"I'm not serving anyone – I just want to find out

what's going on!" Ignoring the pig's disapproving look, I dipped the pen once more in the ink and scratched out:

Hi.

I drew a speech balloon round it and stepped back, watching the blank panel next door on the moonlit page, full of anticipation, waiting for something to happen.

And within a couple of minutes, before my disbelieving eyes, it did.

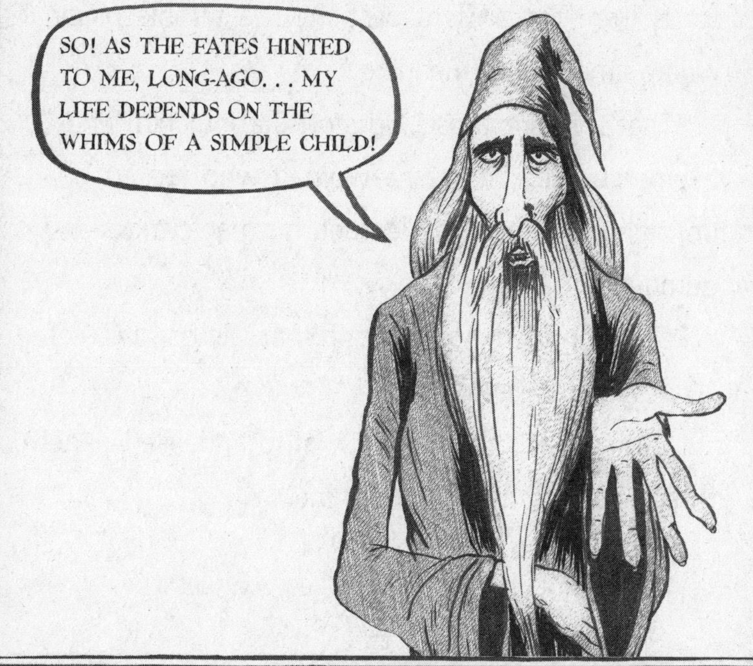

SO! AS THE FATES HINTED TO ME, LONG-AGO. . . MY LIFE DEPENDS ON THE WHIMS OF A SIMPLE CHILD!

CHAP-TO-CHAP-TER THIRTEEN

MERLIN!!!

Merlin's artwork was cool but I wasn't sure about his dialogue. I frowned over at Posho. "Is he calling me simple?"

"I'm sure he merely means 'uncomplicated'," said Posho quickly. "Remember, he's translating his words into English from old Anglo-Saxon. And he's talking to us from the ancient past, from a terrible prison where time has no meaning."

"That's where those old stories about him end," I remembered. "It was a woman who locked him up, right? Viviane. She learned his magic tricks and dumped him."

Posho nodded so hard his hat almost fell off. "A pestilential devil woman!"

I turned back to the comic strip and filled panel three with another picture of me.

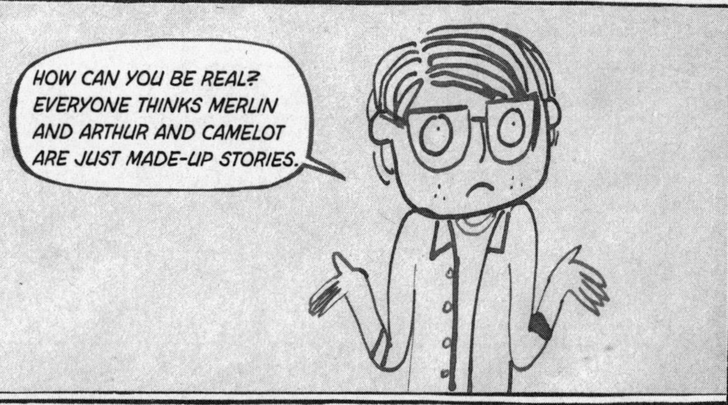

I didn't have to wait long for the next panel to appear.

Posho chuckled. "It rather suits him, doesn't it?"

"Mmm." I didn't want to upset Merlin, so in panel four I drew myself with a big beard and pointy hat as well. What to ask? I had so many questions – like,

If you can send your spirit through time, why do you need me? You say you want to fend off magical attacks – but from who? And is that Viviane woman still after you?

But what was my biggest question? This:

I waited tensely, my eyes glued to the parchment. Well, not literally glued to the parchment. That would hurt. Merlin was good; he came back at me with two panels.

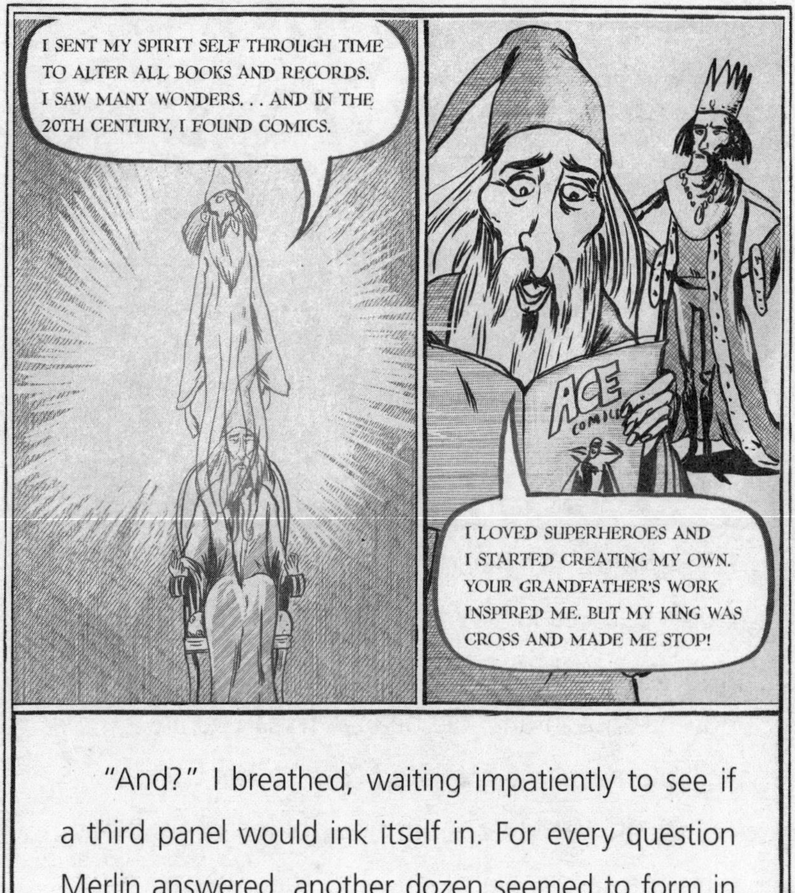

I SENT MY SPIRIT SELF THROUGH TIME TO ALTER ALL BOOKS AND RECORDS. I SAW MANY WONDERS. . . AND IN THE 20TH CENTURY, I FOUND COMICS.

ACE COMICS

I LOVED SUPERHEROES AND I STARTED CREATING MY OWN. YOUR GRANDFATHER'S WORK INSPIRED ME. BUT MY KING WAS CROSS AND MADE ME STOP!

"And?" I breathed, waiting impatiently to see if a third panel would ink itself in. For every question Merlin answered, another dozen seemed to form in my reeling mind.

Then I forgot them all, as another image came through. It was a little sketchier than the first two. And the scene it showed gave me the creeps.

If this was a proper self-portrait, then Merlin really *was* in trouble.

NOW I AM TRAPPED. ONLY THE GREATEST SUPERHEROES CAN SET ME FREE! YOUR DRAWING SHOWS PROMISE, LAD. I HAVE BUT ONE CHANCE TO ESCAPE. . . . HELP ME AND I SHALL REWARD YOU WELL!

"Reward?" My heart quickened. "What reward?" I looked at Posho. "What does he mean, 'reward'?"

"I don't know." The pig looked kind of rueful. *"I'm* not the chosen one, old bean. **Oink!** You are."

"You mean, my granddad was," I shot back.

"Oink! Well, yes – but now, blood of his blood, with the same love of drawing superheroes, you're the closest thing to the chosen one the Big Man has."

"But if he can travel through time, why does he need me?"

"You heard him, old boy," said Posho shortly. "His spirit self was able to flit across the centuries but the real him had to stay put. **Oink!** Now, locked up as he is, only his artwork can escape – carried on moonlight and drawn here through the ink-link. You alone can help him now!"

My mind was whirling. Me, Stew Penders, comics geek, a chosen one! Chosen by fate – and by a mythical wizard. I could almost hear the ancient scratch of Merlin's fading whispers, like the rasping of a pen nib on parchment. . .

Was I going to wimp out like Granddad? Run away? Let the chance go? Let the *reward* go?

I found myself hastily scribbling a heroic silhouette – one fist raised to the sky above him. It was me – as ***STUPENDOUS MAN.***

I stared at the freaky tag-team comic strip conversation I'd just taken part in, while Posho taped another blank-panelled page to the drawing board.

Together we waited for Merlin's reaction. My stomach churned like a washing machine, my guts tossing like laundry.

But as the minutes passed, my excitement ebbed. The next panel remained blank.

Unknown.

Like the future. . .

CHAPTER FOR TEEN

(AND FOR ANYONE WHO'S NOT A TEEN BUT WHO MIGHT WANT TO READ IT ANYWAY. PARTICULARLY ANYONE INTERESTED IN MEDIEVAL SUPERHEROES)

Posho and I waited for several minutes for any further message from Merlin. You know, like a 'Thanks, mate!' or 'Cheers!' But nothing came through. Even the smears on my finger and thumb had grown faint.

"Er… Why has he stopped talking?" I whispered.

"**Oink!** You saw that picture. He's in a bad way." Posho sighed. "We'll try to reach him again tomorrow night. We must find out which superhero he needs."

He needs Stupendous Man, I thought to myself, boggling at the prospect of my super-charged alter-ego springing to life in the moonlight. "Hang on, though, why can't Merlin just magic himself out of that cave?"

"There are many barriers around it, both magical and physical, which can only be broken from the outside," said Posho gravely. "But it's late now.

Oink! I'll clue you in on all the details tomorrow."

"Right. . . " I looked at the dapper pig. "Posho, if my granddad drew you into life and then ran off, how come you know so much about Merlin's situation?"

"Er. . . Well, I was made with Merlin's magic, wasn't I?" Posho looked a bit shifty. "**Oink!** I'm here to help him find a hero in his time of need! His right-hand pig, you could say. Now, no more questions, old bean. Off you go, and take some Magic, Inc. comics with you. You must get as acquainted with the Big Man's creations as a piglet with its litter-mates' tails."

I picked up the bundle of yellowed pages from the table. "All right. See you tomorrow."

"**Oink!** Toodle-pip!"

Quietly, I crept out of the moonlit attic and down the stairs. I could hear Mum and Dad softly snoring in unison, and Libs grinding her teeth in her sleep. Again, I felt shut out of that ordinary, careless world, with my secrets and my bargains, my late-night promises and my talking pig. . .

As I pulled the sheets over me, I thought, 'What have I got myself into?' Had I said yes to Merlin for the right reasons? I realised, kind of guiltily, that the thought of a magical reward had definitely helped persuade me. And yet I didn't even know what the reward would be.

Money?

Special powers?

My mind skipped and skidded around the possibilities.

To try and calm myself down I started looking through the comics. Though the smudge on my thumb was fainter than before, by wiping it across the words I could still make sense of most of them.

And I came to the conclusion that Magic, Inc.'s superheroes were a pretty weird bunch.

Obviously, things were different back in Merlin's day – and his costumed characters reflected this.

There was. . .

The hay-mazing ***HARVEST BOY***, with the unnerving ability to gather one million turnips an hour! **THRILL** as he reaps an entire wheat field in seventeen minutes flat! **GASP** as he tills the soil with his bare hands! **BLINK IN DISBELIEF** as he leaves harvested potatoes out in the sun for a while to harden their skins so they store better!

In ***Harvest Boy*** Issue 1, Harvest Boy helped the women and children of a village gather in their harvest while the men were away fighting in a war. It wasn't really that exciting. Except for the women and children in the story, who got a nice couple of days off thanks to their helpful hero being so efficient.

Another of the weird old comics was the first issue of ***The Living Trebuchet***. Now, I'd been on a school trip to a castle the year before so I knew a trebuchet was a giant catapult that propelled big rocks at big buildings to try and knock them down. And I was pretty sure that most trebuchets were dead, being made of wood and stuff.

So what was a living trebuchet?

The answer was…

SONNY SIEGE, a teenage boy who was apparently King Arthur's ultimate weapon against enemy nobles. His super-powers were amazing strength, resistance to disease and the ability to fling rotting cows and horses over the top of a castle wall to try and spread illnesses.

STARE as he summons zombie plague-rats from the dead to attack people! **HOLD YOUR STOMACH** as he tricks the population of an entire castle into drinking water infected with cholera (or something) so they all die and King Arthur can breeze in and take over!

Nice, huh? Wonder if any of these mags made it to issue two?

My eyes were starting to droop by now. You might be wondering, how could I feel sleepy after seeing all that craziness? After translating old languages with an inky thumb?

Well, once you're forced to accept that this mad stuff is real, that's about it. You can't deny it any more, so you just get on with it.

And you get yourself in deeper.

I decided to flick through the ***War Commander*** comic.

It was about a knight called Lance Lott who seemed to mainly fight Vikings and warlords who bad-mouthed Arthur. This was a bit more like it.

Last on the pile was ***The Adventures of Lantern Girl***, Issue 1 – and it was perhaps the weakest comic of all.

Lantern Girl was an orphan who'd been bitten by a radioactive glow-worm (which seemed kind of unlikely to me, as there wasn't any harmful radiation back then, was there? And can worms bite? I don't think so.)

She had the power to make her hand glow brightly.

I mean, OK, I guess back in those days before electricity, a bit of extra light would come in handy but. . . Well. A glowing hand for a superpower? *Really?* Wow.

YELP IN SHOCK as she helps a monk finish writing his book after his candles have been stolen. **GAZE IN AWE** as she illuminates a forest track so a messenger on horseback doesn't stumble into a small hole. . .

I ended up sleeping very well indeed that night.

CHAPTER FFFIFTEEEN

TO THE SUPERMARKET!

(or, EXCUSE ME, there's a wizard in my potatoes)

I woke the next morning with Merlin and his prison on my mind and fear and excitement swilling about in my stomach. But before I could sneak upstairs to get more info from Posho, Mum intervened – and forced me to go with her to the supermarket in town. Not Lib, who got to stay home with Dad watching TV – just me, so I could push the trolley for her. Mum knew better than to bring both of us on a shopping trip. Things normally worked out badly.

Anyway, I was standing in the fruit and veg section while Mum poked about at some cherry tomatoes, when suddenly I saw a cloud of smoke come billowing through the air towards me. Before I could react—

WHOOSH!

A tall, bearded man in a dark cloak and pointy hat appeared, standing on the potatoes in the weigh-your-

own section! I staggered back, trying to scream, but my voice had shrivelled to a croaking whisper. . .

"Don't be a-feared, boy," the man in the potatoes said kindly, his voice rich and deep. "I am the wizard Merlin, here in my astral form. Only you can see me!"

"H. . . huh?" I whimpered. "How come you didn't just appear like that last night?"

"Last night?" Merlin frowned. "Ah. No. No, no, no, boy. I am not the same Merlin you must have spoken to. I am an earlier, younger version, still at liberty, acting on special instructions. You see?"

"Er. . . not really, no," I said, not believing my eyes – let alone my ears. As I watched, an old woman wandered over and helped herself to a handful of the potatoes under the apparition's bare and dirty feet *(euww!)* without comment. And no one else was so much as glancing at the strange, slightly transparent, cowled figure standing on the veg. They were looking at ME – flippin' cheek! – as if I were the only weird thing around here!

"A younger Merlin. . ." I breathed. "Then. . . the Merlin I spoke to is still a prisoner?"

"Eh? Prisoner of what?" Merlin frowned. "No! Don't answer that. Speak not a word of whatever has already passed between us – for you, it is in the past, for me, it is still to come in the future. What you see before you now is but my spirit self – an intangible shadow of the real me, projected through the ages by the power of my mind."

I groped around in my own mind for something intelligent to say. "Uhh. . . why are you in a supermarket?"

"This is the time and place I was told I would find you," Merlin began.

"Told by who?" I asked.

"Stop interrupting, lad!" Merlin grumbled. "You see, before me there lies a—"

"Grapefruit!" said Mum, bustling back over with

the tomatoes. "We need a grapefruit. End of the aisle. Come on, Stew, stop staring into space and get with it!"

I couldn't believe that my senses-staggering conversation with the one and only actual Merlin was being interrupted by a grapefruit. With a helpless look at the ghostly wizard, I wheeled the trolley off after Mum.

As we reached the end of the aisle, Merlin appeared again – this time on the cereal counter opposite the grapefruits. His insubstantial form was perched impressively on a stack of Golden Nuggets. I tried hard not to stare so that Mum wouldn't get mad, but it was difficult.

"As I was saying," Merlin went on patiently, "before me there lies a great and terrible challenge. I sense that I will soon be struggling for my very life."

"But if you can travel into the future," I broke in quietly, "can't you see what happens and avoid it?"

"Sadly not," said Merlin. "That is impossible because of—"

"Nectarines," said Mum, striding off. "Come on.

Stop talking to yourself!"

I looked across at the magician on his seat of cereal. "Maybe we should talk some other time?" I hissed. "How can I even understand you, anyway? Your comics were in Latin."

Merlin tutted. "I'm a wizard, lad! I have sent this astral projection of myself across fifteen centuries to track you down, haven't I? I mastered your modern language long ago so I could enjoy the marvellous comics made by the likes of Stan Lee and Roy Thomas and Jack Kirby and Garry Penders. . ."

"My granddad!" I whispered in a daze.

"Really?" Merlin's eyes lit up. "Is he around here? Can I get his autograph?"

"Um, no – he passed away a couple of months ago."

The big man groaned – and then, so did Mum. "Stew, come ON!" She looked like she might go fairly nuclear sometime soon.

"Er. . . sorry." I said it to her, but meant it for Merlin.

However, it seemed the ghostly mage wasn't about to be put off. With a swirl of mist, he reappeared beside the nectarines. How did he find them so fast, and tell them apart from the peaches? Clearly, he really **WAS** magic!

I smiled politely. "You, er, were telling me why it's impossible for you to learn your destiny. . ."

"I tried to peek once," Merlin confessed. "It was no good. The view is clouded with dark spells that can only have been cast by some fearsome future foe. That is how I know there is a struggle ahead. Now, my lad—"

"Tights!" Mum cried suddenly, placing a punnet of nectarines into the trolley. "I almost forgot, I have to buy some more tights, all mine have gone missing. Wait for me by the pasta, Stew, while I nip and get them. Oh, I've just got too much to cope with. . ."

As she walked away, Merlin vanished once more – only to reappear in the trolley's toddler seat!

"What is this pasta of which your matriarch speaks?" the great wizard enquired.

"Uh, just food. From Italy." I gingerly returned to pushing the trolley, trying not to let the wizard's ghostly feet brush through my legs. "You know, this is totally weird!"

"In truth, I too am perturbed." Merlin looked all around. "You mean to say, this place is a store for foods harvested from around the world? You must surely have your own Harvest Boy in this time, to gather so many."

"Harvest Boy as in your, uh, 'superhero', you mean?" I felt kind of awkward. "Er, no. Superheroes aren't real."

"Mine were," Merlin said calmly, fixing me with his gaze. "In my own time, heroes of greatness were sorely needed. So, inspired by the comics of this time, I started Magic, Inc. - my own comics company. I created my own characters and brought them to magical life. . ."

"Like Posho," I breathed, as we turned into the pasta aisle.

"Posh what? No! Don't tell me." Merlin suddenly yelled, "**La-la-la-la!**" and covered his ears. I couldn't believe the crowds around me were deaf to it all; as deaf as Merlin, it seemed. "Can't hear a thing when I do this," the magician went on cheerily. "**La-la-la-la!** I do it when Arthur's making speeches sometimes – he hates it, ha ha! Perhaps I should've been a singer. . ."

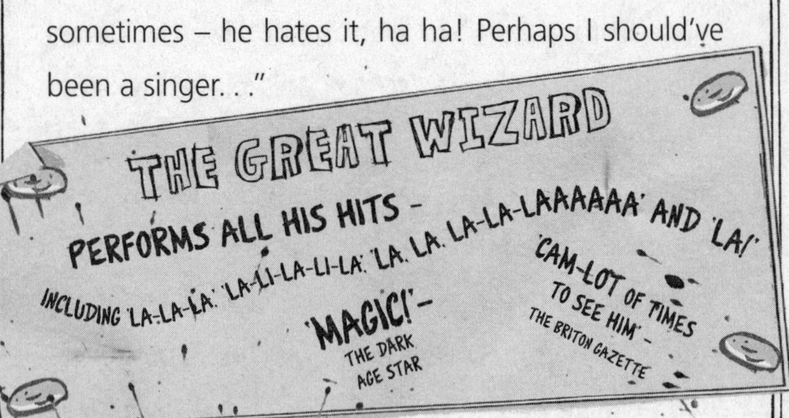

THE GREAT WIZARD
PERFORMS ALL HIS HITS –
INCLUDING 'LA-LA-LA', 'LA-LI-LA-LI-LA', 'LA. LA. LA-LA-LA-LAAAAAA' AND 'LA!'
'MAGIC!' – THE DARK AGE STAR
'CAM-LOT OF TIMES TO SEE HIM' – THE BRITON GAZETTE

"Merlin," I whispered, as he finally removed his fingers from his ears. "Back-tracking a bit, do you mean that Lantern Girl and Sonny Siege and War Commander really were alive?"

"Alive and fit for fighting and wrong-righting. My comics were not fiction as are your modern comics, but a true chronicle of my heroes' brave and bold actions all over Arthur's kingdom." The wizard's face darkened. "Arthur's kingdom, yes – he never let me forget it! That strutting peacock couldn't handle the competition my characters gave him! Arthur wanted to be the only hero in the land. . . so he demanded I stop conjuring superheroes and stop making comics."

I brought the trolley to a rest beside the spaghetti. "That's. . . that's tough."

The wizard's eyes seemed wet with tears. "Arthur made me close down Magic, Inc. and return to my proper wizardly duties as his guide and mentor. I had to give up on my comics empire, just because he said so. . . oh, and because there were no such things as printing presses or paper. . . And because the population couldn't read. Lame excuses!"

They actually sounded quite good excuses to me.

"In any case. . ." The wizard cleared his throat noisily. "My mission here today is to reveal this to you: that, if you succeed in whatever great service you have sworn to perform for me, I will reward you handsomely. . ."

I gulped again. "Handsomely?"

"Extremely handsomely. . ." Merlin raised an eyebrow and smiled. "I shall revive my magical comics company in this century. I shall put you in direct control of Magic, Inc.!"

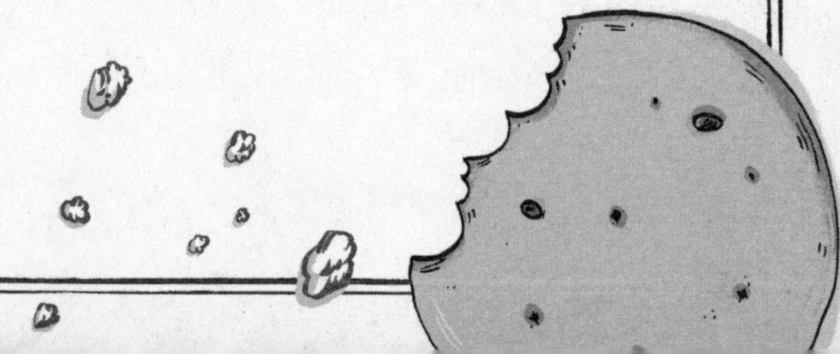

THE SIXTEENTH CHAPTRE

FROM THE SUPERMARKET TO. . . SOMEWHERE ELSE

(Possibly back home. Ok, yes, straight home. Well, what did you expect? It was raining!)

You can picture me, can't you, at that moment in the supermarket, as Merlin dropped his bombshell beside the pasta sauces. "Magic, Inc.," I breathed, every sense in shock, every moment stretching into infinity as the words sunk in.

I must have stayed like that for maybe half a second. Then I frowned.

"But. . . I'm still at school," I whispered, ignoring the look an old lady was giving me as she reached for a jar of Bolognese sauce. "I can't control a business. What kind of a reward is that?"

"Magic, Inc. will give you great advantage in the world of comics. Especially once you have this." Merlin pulled a slim, neat, beautifully made paintbrush from inside his sleeve. And unlike the rest of Merlin, it was solid and real. He pressed the brush into my hand, and little prickles of power sparked through my fingers.

I can help your talents grow, he'd told me yesterday.

"When dipped in the magic ink that you already possess, and when in close proximity to the drawing board of a master comic-book artist like your grandfather, this charmed instrument will allow you to draw as well as the finest comics artist you can imagine. Your work will be admired and desired by many companies. You will become famous and wealthy – that shall be your reward! And once you are full-grown you will be able to start your own comics empire. A mighty empire that, in honour of old Merlin and his lofty ambitions, you shall name—"

"Frozen pizzas," Mum announced, making me jump half a mile.

Merlin glared at her. "That is a rubbish name, Madam!"

She couldn't hear him, of course. "We need to get pizza for dinner tonight, Stew." I hid the brush behind my back and stuffed it down the back of my trousers as she chucked a packet of tights into the trolley and bustled away. "Come on, get wheeling."

Merlin tutted as I pushed the trolley after Mum.

"I'm sorry about her," I said. "I'm sure if she could see you she wouldn't keep interrupting. She'd just faint or something." Thing was, I felt close to fainting myself. My brain was ablaze with the fabulous futures that suddenly seemed possible. "My own comics empire. . . My 'Magic, Inc.'. . ." My cheeks ached with the size of the grin on my face. "Thank you, great wizard. Thank you so much."

"Thank you, for whatever it is you will do for me." Merlin looked troubled. "I fear that for me to grant you such a prize as this, the needs of my future self must be mighty indeed."

"You sure you don't want me to tell you about the—?"

"La-la-la-la!" Merlin shook his head so hard that his pointy hat nearly flew off and stabbed an old lady in the eye. "Now, my spirit's time in your strange world is coming to an end. I must return to my waiting body in my own time of 500 AD." He gave me a cheerless smile. "Farewell, lad. May we both be equal to the challenges ahead. . ."

"Thank you, sir." I stared, transfixed, as the wizard's apparition dissolved into scentless smoke. "I'll try my best, I'll—"

"OWW!" Mum rubbed her behind and grimaced. "You banged the trolley into my bottom, Stew! You're away with the fairies today – honestly, I wish I'd left you at home!"

"Sorry, Mum. Perhaps you could take me back right now, and finish the shopping on your own later?" I suggested.

The look she gave me suggested 'perhaps not'. Still, it had been worth a try. Merlin's mysterious brush was burning a hole in the back of my pants. Not literally – that wouldn't be cool. It would be hot. What I mean is, I couldn't wait to get using it.

I'm going to be rich! I thought, staring fervently at Merlin's gift every chance I could. Perhaps it was a good thing that all my friends were fifty miles away or I might've blabbed to one of them, giving away my new secret identity as Merlin's Rescuer-to-be.

I was dying to sneak up to the attic and try out my brand new brush at Granddad's drawing board, as Merlin had directed. But I didn't want to be disturbed, so I forced myself to wait for the perfect opportunity...

As a result, the day lasted about forever.

I did your normal, boring kind of stuff – you know, putting away the groceries, grabbing some toast for lunch, accidentally getting Lib in a headlock and throwing her onto the sofa, blah blah blah. To be honest, I wasn't really that interested in tormenting Lib, but I knew that it was a surefire way of getting sent to my room – and from there, it was a whole lot easier to slip away upstairs to the attic.

So around late afternoon I 'accidentally' stepped on her mermaid picnic, got myself a wail from Lib and a telling-off from Mum, and duly trooped away upstairs – to the top of the house, brand new ancient brush in hand.

"Posho?" I whispered, slowly opening the door.

SPLOSH! A carefully placed plastic bucket

of water fell onto my head, drenching me in a moment. The oldest practical joke in the book!

It was all I could do not to yell out in shock – at which point Mum and Dad would've come charging upstairs to sort me out. As it was, I suppose it was lucky my head had caught the bucket before it could thump onto the floor – if you can call that luck.

"Posho, what are you playing at?!" I hissed.

"Sorry, old bean!" The upper crust pig peered out apologetically from behind the armchair. "**Oink!** I simply couldn't help myself. I'm made this way! Goodness knows, I've tried to change. . . I'd love to be better than this, you know."

To my surprise, he really did look upset.

"Look at me," I muttered. "I'm soaked."

"I took a towel from the bathroom so you could dry off. It's on the stool there." Posho tutted. "Where have you been, anyway?"

"I had to go out. And you'll never guess who I saw." Despite my soaking, I couldn't help but grin. "The Big Man! It was kind of a spirit version of Merlin, an earlier him from before he was captured. . ."

"Pardon? PARDON?" Posho came scampering towards me, his eyes wide and bright, his top hat

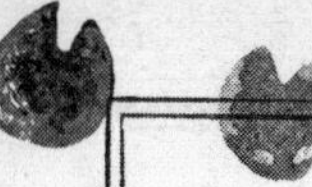

barely clinging to his ears. "You actually talked with the Big Man IN PERSON?"

"Yeah!" I shook my head, marvelling. "I mean, I don't know how Merlin knew to come and see me before Viviane locked him up," I said. "But it sounds like he can see into the future a little bit, even if he isn't meant to. He is a wizard, after all."

"I do hope so." Posho clapped his trotters together. "Tell me more, tell me more. . ."

As I filled in Posho on all that had happened, I couldn't help but notice his corkscrew tail growing limper, as the crestfallen look returned to his piggy face.

"If only I'd been there," he said quietly. "Twenty years I've been waiting and wanting to help the Big Man."

"You have," I told him. "I mean, if you hadn't been here, I'd never have worked out what to do. How the flip did my granddad even know to draw on the magic paper?"

"Oink! Instructions were left, old fruit – buried in your grandfather's garden along with the Magic, Inc.

comics." Posho sighed deeply. "After I sprang to life, the old boy tried to burn the lot. I salvaged all I could – he didn't realise I could get out of the attic. I don't think he ever truly believed I was real at all."

"You did brilliantly," I said kindly. "Now, could I see all those instructions? Especially any stuff about the prison itself?"

"Eh? Oh. . . yes. The Big Man told your grandfather all about it when they began their brief acquaintance." Posho looked shifty. "**Oink!** I'll fetch them. But first you must stand in the corner and hide your eyes."

I blinked. "Why?"

"It's, er, part of the magic," Posho insisted.

I did as he said.

But obviously I peeped a little bit.

And I saw Posho scurry over to his favourite part of the attic and pull up a floorboard. So that was where he kept Merlin's stuff! I had to admit, here was a pig who planned for every possibility. He was sneakier than he seemed.

I couldn't see exactly what he was up to in the space beneath the floorboard, but soon he was treading it back into place and turning back to me with a roll of parchment.

"There." He pressed it into my hand. "This rescue will be quite a challenge, as you can see."

And as I opened my eyes, I could see. Boy, could I see.

I just didn't really want to.

There, in scratchy letters – along with a few off-putting illustrations – was the list of defences around the cave. It read:

KNOW YE, GARRY, THE HORRORS THAT AWAIT ALL WHO DARE VENTURE CLOSE TO THE PRISON TOMB OF MERLIN

• A GREAT DRAGON DOTH STAND GUARD AT THE ENTRANCE WITH FIERY BREATH AND POISONOUS CLAWS.

• THE FEARSOME BULK OF THE GREAT DRAGON DOTH RESIDE IN A DANK HELLISH PIT IN WHICH LURKS A HORDE OF DEMONIC SKELETON WARRIORS.

YES! I AM THE SAME DRAGON AS THE ONE ON THE BACK COVER!
WE'LL HAVE YOU! MAKE NO BONES ABOUT IT!

• AT THE BACK OF THE PIT THERE STANDS A FORBIDDEN DOOR THAT LEADS TO THE WATERS OF A WRETCHEDLY EVIL AND OVERWEIGHT SIREN – A DANGEROUS, DEVIOUS WOMAN-WRAITH WHO WILL PUT THE FOOLISH WOULD-BE-RESCUER TO ETERNAL SLEEP WITH HER UNEARTHLY SONG.

I LIKE A GOOD SING-SONG, ME!

• BEHIND THE SIREN IS AN ENORMOUS BLOCK OF LIMESTONE THAT SEALS THE ENTRANCE TO THAT BLIGHTED CAVE WHEREIN I HAVE BEEN LEFT TO ROT LIKE A MAGGOTY WORM.

I'M AN INANIMATE OBJECT, I HAVE NOTHING TO SAY.

KNOW TOO, GARRY PENDERS, THAT I HAVE BUT ONE CHANCE TO ESCAPE. THE LADY VIVIANE, MY DIVINE NEMESIS, HAS PROMISED THAT SHOULD SHE DETECT AN INTRUDER ATTEMPTING TO INFILTRATE THESE DEFENCES, SHE WILL RETURN SWIFTLY TO DESTROY ME HERSELF. SO, IF A RESCUE IS TO BE LAUNCHED, IT MUST TAKE PLACE AT GREAT SPEED – OR ELSE YOU WILL SUCCEED ONLY IN FREEING MY CHARRED AND HIDEOUSLY MUTILATED CORPSE!

IN THE HOPE THAT YOU WILL NOT BE DETERRED, I REMAIN

YOURS OPTIMISTICALLY

Merlin

XX

CHAPTER SEVENTOON

DRAWING ON ALL MY RESERVES OF. . . ER, DRAWING

"Wow." I lowered the parchment with a shaky hand. "Those defences sound pretty hardcore."

"And now, you must do what your grandfather chose not to do. **Oink!** You must draw the superhero who can get past them to get the Big Man out." Posho glanced at his favourite floorboard in a furtive fashion. "Or superheroes, perhaps. As in, plural. More than one."

I shook my head. "Stupendous Man works alone."

Posho frowned. "*Who*-pendous man?"

"The superhero I've invented! I've been drawing him, like, for ever!" I gazed down at the magic brush. "He'd be perfect to rescue Merlin."

"I see," said Posho. "Well, tonight, if the night is clear and the moonlight strong – **Oink!** – Merlin will commune with us again and give his instructions."

"I'll welcome him back with a greeting from Stupendous Man," I decided, taking up my place at the drawing board – I just had to try out that brush. "If Merlin was right about what this thing can do, I'll be able to make my characters look like they've been drawn by real comic book artists. . . And the Big Man will know straight away that his magic's worked."

Taking a canyon-deep breath, I dipped the point of my brush in the magic ink. My hand grew suddenly warmer, twitching as if there was an itch inside, and the only way to scratch that itch was. . .

Almost before I knew it, I was drawing – inking Stupendous Man like I was following invisible guides. From this moment, I could forget felt-tips and dump dip pens; each stroke of the brush came out sharp and confident; it seemed I hardly had to move my hand at all. I watched the picture emerge, marvelling, but terrified I might spoil it at any moment, hardly daring even to breathe.

My excitement built and built until finally, there he was – Stupendous Man as I'd always dreamed of seeing him.

His expression screamed raw bravery, his every bulging muscle portrayed in perfect detail. There he stood on the parchment – a truly superhuman hero.

I had left space for a few words in a speech balloon: **THE BRUSH WORKS WELL. . . NOW, TO THE RESCUE!** The bold letters sped from the tip of the brush. I inked the oval around them and then dropped the brush back in the bottle of magic ink. My hand felt hot and trembling. I stared at it, wonderingly.

"Good work, old bean," snuffled Posho. "Not bad at all." He was staring at the panel I had filled with perhaps a hint of envy in his eyes. "I'm sure the Big Man will be pleased – that chap looks a match for most types of trouble."

"He is," I agreed. "See, he can draw power from the things around him. If the dragon breathed fire he could absorb it and blast it back, and—"

"Stew. . . ?" Mum was coming up the stairs! "If you're ready to say sorry you can come out of your room and join us. . ."

I froze. Posho looked at me and did a comedy gulp.

"Disaster!" I hissed. "If she finds me up here, soaking wet, with all this water over the floor, she'll hit the roof. She'll never let me in the attic again!"

"Leave it to me!" hissed Posho.

Like a porky blur he jumped high into the air, smacking top-hat-first against the skylight – which can't have been quite on the catch as it swung straight upwards. He scrabbled through, quite impressively for a pig, and the skylight swung shut behind him. I heard his trotters *rat-a-tatting* over the roof, but it was Mum's heavy tread as she scaled the stairs that fixed me where I stood. It's all going to come out, I thought helplessly. The magic ink, the brush, the parchment, Posho, all these secrets—

KER-KRANNG-BLANNG-GSHINK!

I jumped – it sounded like a billion bottles had just fallen from a great height to shatter outside the front door. Mum gasped with surprise, reversed and zoomed right back down the stairs to see what had happened.

"Nigel, what was that?" she yelled over Libby's shrieks of alarm.

Dad was already flinging open the front door. "It sounded like a billion bottles falling from a great height and shattering just outside!"

See?

"I can feel one of my heads coming on," Mum groaned, as she picked up Libby and followed Dad outside.

Posho must've done something to buy me time, I realised. I'd better get spending that time – fast!

On wobbly legs I sprinted down the stairs to the landing, grabbed a towel from the bathroom, sprinted back up the stairs, mopped up the wet patch on the attic carpet, started to sprint back down the stairs, tripped and fell the last several stairs, banged my head on the landing wall, gasped and clutched my head, muttered rude words under my breath, staggered up, got inside my bedroom, tripped over a box of comics, narrowly avoided falling on a near mint copy of *Conan the Barbarian* Issue Eight, fell on my face instead, muttered some even ruder words under my breath, quickly changed out of my wet clothes, chucked them under my duvet, scrambled into some dry clothes, ran from my room and. . .

Bumped straight into Posho, back again – his top hat askew and looking very pleased with himself. "Not a bad distraction, eh, old bean?"

"That was amazing," I told him. "You were, like, an action hero pig just then."

"A hero, you say?" Posho looked super-delighted, and grabbed me in a big, bristly hug. "Thank you! **Oink!** Thank you, dear boy, from the hearty bottom of my bottom-most heart!"

"No worries," I muttered awkwardly. "What did you actually *do,* anyway?" I ran to the window overlooking the front of the house at the far end of the landing.

And gasped.

There, below, were Mum, Dad and Lib, staring at a jagged explosion of broken glass that stretched right across the street. Some of our neighbours had come out to see, and everyone was taking it in turns to shrug, stare down at the road and then up again at the evening sky, over and over again. It looked a bit like a particularly rubbish dance routine.

"The bottles, they. . . they must've fallen from a plane or something," I heard Dad say.

"Or from the roof, of course!" Posho chuckled. "I've been collecting bottles left out for recycling over the last ten-or-so years and storing them in several crates tied up together on the roof. **Oink!** Heaved them all overboard to draw everyone's attention to the front of the house! I was planning to drop them beside the postman one day. It's a shame I shan't get to see the look on his face, but at least all that effort wasn't in vain!"

I looked at him. "Did you check there was no one down below? You might've killed them!"

"Of course I checked!" Posho blustered, fiddling with his moustache. "In any case – **Oink!** – may I remind you that we are engaged in a matter of life and death, old boy?"

I nodded slowly. I was still ecstatic about my amazing drawing upstairs – the first of thousands, it seemed, that would make me rich and famous and a comic book legend. . .

But at what price?

I was starting to realise that this magic stuff wasn't just fun and games. It could be dangerous.

As I'd find out later, it could be deadly dangerous.

"Now, go to your family before you are missed," Posho urged me. "And join me again in the attic later tonight. **Oink!** Toodle-pip!"

As Posho scampered back up to the attic, I staggered downstairs. My family was still huddled together outside the front door.

"This mess'll need clearing up before someone hurts themselves." Dad sounded shell-shocked. "Should we call the council? Or the police?"

"Or the army," said Lib (dumbly, as per usual).

"Or an ambulance," Mum cried, "to take me to hospital when my nerves give up completely!"

And for once, I didn't roll my eyes and grumble. Because, for once, standing there forgotten in the hall, I kind of knew how Mum felt.

CHAPTER EIGHTEEN

POSHO FALLS FROM GRACE

(AND A WINDOW)

(Hang on, have I actually spelled both those wurds korectly?)

As it turns out – and luckily for my guilt levels – Posho's crazy stunt actually did a lot more good than harm for my family. Yeah, sure, it meant a load of grown-ups had to go out with gloves and brooms and dustpans and stuff to clear up the glass before little kids like Lib could go out and fall on it, but it turned out to be a really good way for Mum and Dad to meet the neighbours. I reckon grown-ups secretly like it when stuff goes wrong; they can have a good moan about it together and, like, bond over it. Weirdos.

The bad news was, while Mum and Dad cleared away the remains of the pig's prank, I had to babysit Lib while she babysat for her dolls. And all I could think of, all that mattered to me just then, was getting back upstairs to the attic. I was dying to know what Merlin thought of my artwork. I wanted to start helping him so I could get on with the rest of my now-surely-guaranteed-to-be-fantastic life.

After the big clear-up, Mum and Dad invited some of the neighbours round for tea or something. They were soon all loud voices and hearty laughter, so I guessed there was less tea and more something else quenching their thirst. Mum came up looking flushed and with a red nose, but she wasn't complaining for once; she just wanted me and Lib in bed ASAP so she could get back to the party. Which suited me! As soon as the coast was clear, I snuck up to that magical moonlit room at the top of the house and carefully pushed open the door before I entered. No practical jokes this time. Posho was standing by the drawing board, looking grave.

"I'm glad you're here, old boy," Posho said. "The Big Man has made his feelings clear."

I joined him and found that Merlin had filled a couple of panels already with his long-distance blend of words and pictures:

YOU ARE DRAWING WELL - BUT YOU MUST DRAW MY HEROES, BOY! ALL FOUR, TOGETHER FOR THE FIRST TIME!
ONLY BY WORKING TOGETHER CAN THEY TRIUMPH OVER THE DANGERS AHEAD!

So. Not a single comment on Stupendous Man. "You were right, Posho," I muttered. "It's superheroes he's after, just as you said."

"This team-up wasn't exactly what I had in mind." Posho glanced forlornly at his favourite floorboard again. "**Oink!** Still, if the Big Man favours a super-group of his own heroes, well – he knows best."

"Does he?" I wondered, thinking back to early issues of *The Avengers* comic – and the movie version too. "When you stick a load of superheroes together, they always fight. And anyway, Merlin doesn't know what Stupendous Man can do," I argued. "So. . . I'll show him." I picked up the brush and set to work at once. The sound of merry adults laughing rose from that whole other world downstairs.

The world I was starting to leave behind.

I drew a stonkingly stupendous Stupendous Man, pictured in action against those terrible guardian monsters. My brushstrokes in the magic ink captured each figure deftly and surely; all I had to do was picture the image in my head and the brush would help me to draw it with absolute confidence.

With the picture drawn, I started lettering, trying to sell Merlin on the concept.

IT TAKES SUPERHEROES TIME TO WORK AS A TEAM – MY STUPENDOUS MAN IS TOUGH ENOUGH TO TRIUMPH ON HIS OWN! HE SUCKS IN POWERS FROM THE WORLD AROUND HIM TO USE AGAINST HIS ENEMIES...
SM

I waited eagerly. But as the next panel began to appear, I didn't like it much.

NO, LAD – MY LIFE IS IN THE BALANCE. PLEASE, DO THINGS MY WAY WITH MY HEROES!

Ouch. I felt like a schoolboy who'd picked a fight with the Head Teacher. If Merlin wanted his own heroes, I'd just have to draw them as best I could.

"How's Merlin going to get these characters back to him through time, anyway?" I muttered.

Posho forced a smile. "The Big Man supplied me – er, your grandfather – with a Spell of Time Transportation. **Oink!** It will allow those freshly-drawn heroes to traverse the centuries to the glorious battle that awaits them."

I nodded, still feeling kind of disappointed. And the sixth and seventh panels inked themselves into existence.

YOU SPEAK WISELY OF THE WAY HEROES TAKE TIME TO WORK TOGETHER. I RECALL THE AVENGERS WERE QUITE PRICKLY AT FIRST. YOU MUST HELP MY HEROES TO FIGHT AS A TEAM.

ALAS, THE STRENGTH OF MY MAGIC IS DWINDLING.
ONCE MOONLIGHT BRINGS YOUR DRAWINGS TO LIFE, THE HEROES WILL LAST BUT AN HOUR. HOWEVER, EACH TIME YOU DRAW THEM AND CONJURE THEM ANEW, THEY WILL RETAIN THEIR MEMORIES. TRAIN THEM WELL.

"But. . . I can't!" I spluttered.

"I can help, old chap!" said Posho eagerly. "**Oink!** I can devise strategies. . . Train them in a couple of piggy-commando moves. . ."

He started to pace up and down. While he wasn't looking, I filled panel eight with words.

HOW COME YOUR SUPERHEROES WILL ONLY LAST AN HOUR? POSHO PIG WAS DRAWN 20 YEARS AGO AND IS STILL HERE. HE'S DYING TO HELP, BY THE WAY.

At once, the final panel on the page began to fill with scratchy linework. The picture was not very pleasant – particularly if you were a pig.

WHAT?! THE ACCURSED PIG PRESUMES TO HELP ME – STILL? HE DROVE GARRY PENDERS AWAY AND WRECKED MY BEST CHANCE OF ESCAPE. HIS VERY EXISTENCE HAS DRAINED MY MAGIC FROM A ONCE-RAGING RIVER TO A TINY TRICKLE!.
OINK

"Oh. 'Accursed'? **Oink-oink!** Oh, Merlin!" Beside me, Posho was staring at the parchment, tears welling in his wide and disbelieving eyes. "I'd hoped that after so long. . ."

And then he started to cry. Noisily. Very noisily.

"Posho, don't! Please!" The sight of him so upset was upsetting me. What was worse, because Posho had started life as a cartoon character, he wept like one too – you know, water squirting from his eyes like there were hosepipes hidden inside them. His spurting tears hit me in the face – and splashed all over the drawing board too. The magic ink began to run. "Posho, you're getting the parchment wet!" I spluttered. "I don't know what this is all about, but you need to keep it down! If my mum and dad hear and catch us up here..."

But Posho was inconsolable. He tried to jump out through the skylight again, but his aim was off and it didn't open – he just cracked the pane, his tears like a sprinkler system splashing everything in sight. In desperation I bundled Posho towards the other window and tried to open it so he could cry into the garden instead. The pig was hysterical now, shaking and shuddering and whimpering so hard I could barely hold onto him. He smashed into the window; the catch broke away from the splintering frame and the window opened. . .

"Watch out!" I cried, as the hysterical pig began to tumble backwards over the windowsill. "Don't—"

Too late. Trotters waggling, Posho vanished from sight and went plummeting three storeys down to the ground below.

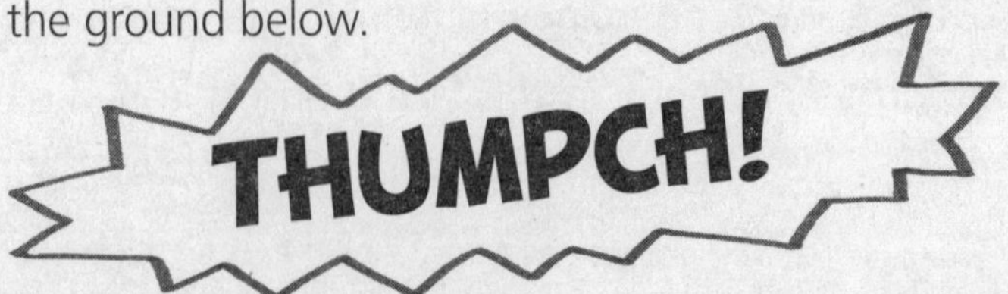

That stopped the pig crying.

The laughter from downstairs now sounded horridly out of place. "Posho!" I hissed anxiously, peering down into the dark space below. Where was the moonlight? Dark clouds in the sky had soaked it up like sponges. I willed my eyes to adapt to the night. "Posho, are you there? Are you all right?"

Only silence answered me. It seemed to last for ever.

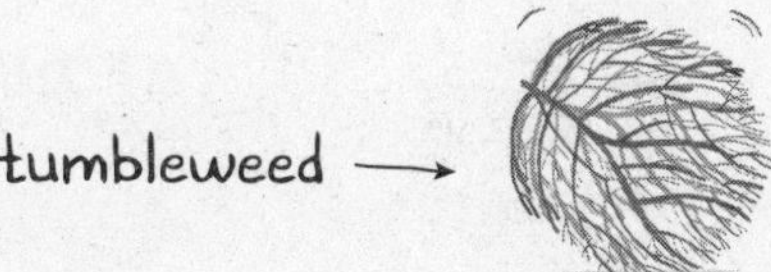

more tumbleweed

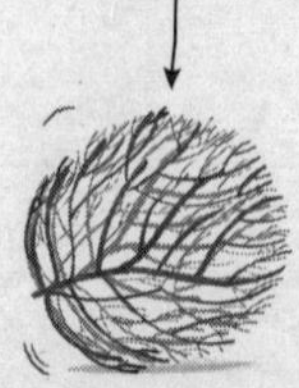

. . . But in fact it only went on for a page and a half.

Then it was followed by a loud sniff and a watery voice: "**Oink!** Dash it. I landed on my top hat – it's ruined!"

I let out a huge sigh of relief. "Posho! Never mind the hat, are you OK?"

He sounded wretched. "I suppose I'm as OK as a presumptuous pig who's been spurned by his master, fallen three floors from an attic window and landed on his head can expect to be. O! Cruel fate. . . what a wretched pig am I. . ."

"I'm glad you're not a terminally squished one." I glared at the paper on the drawing board, which drifted between light and shadow under the cracked skylight, as clouds flitted past the moon.

"Posho never asked to be drawn into existence, Merlin," I muttered. "And as for him messing up your best chance for escape – what am I, then?"

But as the moonlight lingered for a few moments and I saw the desk clearly, I had my answer: You're his last hope, Stew. You're all the Big Man's got.

Where Posho's tears had struck the parchment, Merlin's magic ink had run in washy black dribbles. And the dribbles had formed spidery capital letters. And the letters spelled out these words:

I BEG THEE LAD... HURRY!

CHAPTER NINNIETEEN

WHAT A SURPRISE, THINGS GET COMPLICATED

The night clouds mugged the moon, nicking its light all together before bursting into a downpour of rain, and no moonlight meant no heroes springing to life. So I really couldn't act on Merlin's plea for speed. In any case, poor old Posho was a wreck after the Big Man's outburst, and *I* was a wreck after Posho's burst-out of the window.

The sorry-looking pig hauled himself back up the ivy and into the attic.

"Uh, Posho," I began quietly, "what did Merlin mean, you've drained his—"

"**Oink!** I'd sooner not discuss it right now, old chap." Posho had a big lump on his head, one of those comedy bumps that sticks right up in the air. It made me wonder – could he really hurt himself, or was he as indestructible as most other cartoon characters, like Tom and Jerry or SpongeBob?

Merlin, for all his magic, obviously was NOT indestructible. He really *was* in trouble in that prison of his; I decided that in the circumstances he could be excused a few harsh words.

Of course, if the weather forecast turned properly cloudy for the next few nights, there would be nothing any of us could do to help him. Soon after Posho's dive, the last of the laughing neighbours (a super-jolly couple who made wine from gooseberries called Clarence and Martha – I mean, the neighbours were called Clarence and Martha, not the gooseberries) finally left the house and splashed back next door. And that meant that Mum and Dad might come back upstairs at any moment.

Posho peeled the wet 'talking' parchment from the drawing table. "I'll take care of this," he said dismally. "Pip, pip, old chap. See you tomorrow."

And as the pig returned to his favourite floorboard, I crept back to my room.

Moments later, Mum and Dad came thumping up the stairs, giggling and shushing each other. The secret they were trying to keep: they were a bit tipsy. As for the secrets *I* was trying to keep. . . where to start?

I felt uneasy. Not in control. I mean, besides all the crazy magic stuff (which, weirdly, I was getting used to) someone's life was at stake. And my whole future might be at stake too.

I wasn't surprised when the thunder chose that moment to rumble, like a warning of trouble ahead. And suddenly, I realised that the eerie ink stain had vanished from my finger and thumb. I wondered if it had maybe sunk in through my skin and worked its way up to my brain.

Because the brush and the ink upstairs were all I could think of, the whole night long.

Early the next morning, I was woken by the sound of banging nearby. The rain was still beating on my window, but this sounded more like a hammer. **PAM-PAM-PAMM!**

Hope that's not Dad hitting Posho, I thought in a half-asleep daze. After more efforts at slumber, I gave up and sat in bed with my sketchpad, copying

Merlin's medieval heroes with a felt-tipped pen; good practice, but the pics were like little kids' stuff compared to the pictures I'd drawn in the attic.

I must've drifted off back to sleep again because the next thing I knew, Lib's voice was warbling from downstairs.

"Stew! Breakfast!"

"On my way!"

Despite the grey rainy day, I felt excited. I was itching to get drawing with the super-brush and ink, to take those first steps to rescuing the Big Man…

My good mood lasted all of 65 seconds.

Dad was half dressed, wearing a shirt and his pyjama bottoms. His hair was messed up and he looked pretty rough as he scraped butter across our toast. Mum sat on a stool, spooning down cereal and staring into space.

Something felt odd. This wasn't Normalsville; not anymore.

"Hi," I said. "Wasn't expecting you up so early after your late night. What was that banging I heard?"

Dad grunted. "I've boarded up the windows in the attic."

"WHAT?" The word leaped out of my mouth at ear-exploding volume. Dad dropped his next piece of toast and Lib leaped so high she almost smashed her head through the ceiling.

Mum turned to stare at me. "What's wrong with you?"

"Why did you board them all up?" I demanded.

"The skylight had a crack in it," said Dad. "The frames on the other windows were rotten. One of the catches had broken clean off. Safest to board them up till we get them replaced, stop all this rain getting in."

My heart sank faster than the Titanic with a hundred tap-dancing diplodocuses on board. Dad's handiwork would mean no moonlight could get into the attic – and how would Posho get in and out of the attic unseen?

"You didn't have to board them up," I argued. "Bit of an over-reaction, isn't it?"

Dad smiled. "I don't think so. It's a good chance to do DIY. I love DIY. Don't I, Bryony?"

"Yes, Nigel," said Mum calmly, still staring into space. "You love DIY."

"Er. . . are you two OK?" I asked.

"We'll sort out nice new windows while we're doing up the place," Dad went on, ignoring me. "Your mum and I are going to start clearing out the attic today."

HUH?

The words did not compute. "You're. . . smearing out the Arctic?"

Dad spoke slowly: "We're clearing out the attic."

"You're keeping out a hat-trick?"

"Clearing out the attic," Mum intoned.

"Cleaning up the cat sick?"

"Stew," Lib butted in crossly, "they're going to start clearing out the smelly old attic."

"Wha...aaa...a...?" You can probably imagine the expression on my face. "The attic doesn't need clearing out," I cried. "What about Granddad's stuff?"

"Making a clean start is the healthiest thing to do," said Mum.

Not for Merlin and Posho it isn't, I thought. The attic was our base of operations. I couldn't create four medieval superheroes in my bedroom; there wasn't room and it was way too close to Mum and Dad and Lib. And where would Posho go while the decorating got done? I couldn't be expected to share a room with a pig, even a cartoon one. It would be hopeless.

"Martha and Clarence were telling us last night how they've turned their attic into a very nice guest bedroom," Mum said suddenly. "So we're going to do the same with ours."

"Starting today," Dad announced.

"Today?" I couldn't believe what I was hearing. "Why the rush?"

Dad and Mum both looked at me sharply.

"Why do you care, Stew?" Mum said. "It's not like you ever go in the attic. . . is it?"

I swallowed like there was a lump in my throat. "Er. . . no. But what about Granddad's pictures on the wall?"

"I suppose you can have those," said Mum.

"Can you start decorating straight away?" Lib was almost drooling with enthusiasm. "I could help pick colours."

"Already picked, little darling." Dad smiled. "I got a cheap job lot of 'Fairy Blush' emulsion when we did your room at the old house. We've still got three-and-a-half tins left."

I shook my head in absolute disgust. This was a

disaster. A total disaster. Not only was the Magic, Inc. hideout going to be turned into a spare bedroom, it was going to be PINK!

"Well, if you have to turn Granddad's old office into a girly princess parlour, what about his drawing board? Can I have it in my bedroom?"

Dad shook his head. "There's not enough room for it in there."

"I'll make room," I promised. "Please? If I—"

"No, Stew. We need to sell it." Mum was back to staring vacantly into space. "With all the classic characters Granddad drew there over the years, it's a collector's item. And selling it should make enough money to pay for the new attic furniture. . ."

Now I *really* felt sick. Merlin had said Granddad's drawing board was a vital part of the magical process.

THE MANY PICTURES DRAWN AT GARRY PENDERS' BOARD OVER THE DECADES HAVE LEFT IT STEEPED IN SPECIAL MAGIC – 'CREATIVE ENERGY WAVES' THAT HELP BOND THE ARTIST, THE BRUSH AND INK SO AS TO CREATE CHARACTERS THAT WILL SPRING TO LIFE.

Without the board, I would never be able to pull off what Merlin needed.

"I don't know what you had to drink last night that's turned you so weird this morning," I said, "but you could at least let me keep the drawing board till you find someone to buy it. *Please?*"

"We've already found someone." Dad swapped a knowing smile with Mum. "Turns out Mike across the street has a friend who buys and sells special collectors' items – he wants to come round this evening and take a look at the drawing board—"

"No!" I shouted. "This is totally unfair. **Totally!**"

Leaving my toast uneaten, I stomped upstairs as hard as I could, all the way up to my room. I took my torch, then slammed the door.

But I had slammed it from the *outside,* and now I went creeping up to the attic as fast as my twitching toes would carry me – while I still could.

I had to find Posho and work out what the hecking flip to do next!

CHAPTER TWONTY

INK-REDIBLE SUPERHEROES

(as drawn by me. . .)

It was a lot darker in the attic now the windows were covered up. I ventured into the gloom, shining my torch about. "Posho?" I hissed. "Are you there?" And as I did so, a sneaky thought struck me – this might be my last chance to peek under the floorboard at his secret stash of stuff he'd saved from my granddad's destructive spree of 'this-never-happened-la-la-la'-ness.

I put down the torch and went to work. The length of wood came out easily. The rolls of brown and blackened parchment inside soon followed. First, I found the comic-strip convos I'd been having with Merlin and the big picture of Posho that Granddad had drawn, tucked away for safekeeping. Underneath that I found some partly-burned paper with instructions in fancy handwriting, stating that:

"THE ENCLOSED SUBSTANCES WERE BURIED HEREABOUTS IN 500 AD BY MERLIN THE MAGNIFICENT, AND KNOW YE THEY ARE FOR THE SOLE ATTENTION OF MASTER ARTIST MR GARRY PENDERS. FOR I HAVE PEERED INTO THE FUTURE AND SEEN YOU SHALL SURELY RESIDE HERE IN TIMES LONG HENCE, GARRY, AND THAT YOU SHALL DIG UP THAT UNSIGHTLY LAUREL BUSH AND SO DISCOVER THESE SUBSTANCES SO ENCLOSED (AS MENTIONED) BURIED UNDERNEATH . . . "

I nodded to myself, guessing that while the astral Merlin might be able to deliver something small like a pen to me in person, a stack of parchment and comics and a bottle of magic ink would be a bit much for his ghostly form to carry. He must've had a mystical tip-off, or a tiny peep into the future, and like a good Dark Ages boy scout he had been prepared, burying the stuff for Granddad to find all those centuries later. . .

My head was starting to throb.

What else had Posho salvaged from Granddad's fire and hidden here? I sifted through instructions showing how to use the different types of parchment, then found a busy comic strip on a page underneath.

Prickles went down, along and right through my spine.

It was clearly the fateful first and last conversation between my granddad and the Big Man himself. In the first panel Merlin had drawn himself desperate, eyes wide and pleading.

Granddad had drawn a stick man in response – a stick man broken in half.

I MUST BE CRACKING UP! THINK I'M THE ONE WHO NEEDS HELP! IS THIS A TRICK, OR...?

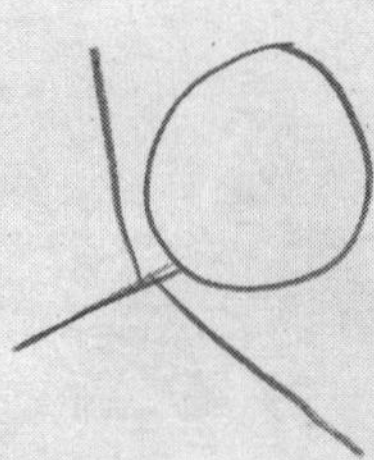

Merlin had then launched straight into his sales pitch, of course:

NO! WHILE YOUR WORLD BELIEVES ME A LEGEND ONLY, I FACE A TERRIBLE FATE COUNTLESS CENTURIES PAST, AND ONLY SUPERHEROES CAN FREE ME.

The Big Man went on for four more panels, begging Granddad to draw the mighty defenders required for the job.

I NEED YOU TO RECREATE MY PROUD WARRIORS IN THIS SPECIAL INK.

WHEN MOONLIGHT TOUCHES THE INK, SUPERHEROES SHALL TRULY WALK YOUR EARTH. AWESOME, HUH?!

YOU CAN SEND THEM BACK THROUGH TIME TO SAVE ME. COOL, DADDIO!

ER, HELLO? MAYHAPS YOU ARE CONSIDERING MY OFFER?

But there was no picture back from my granddad. Just a hasty scrawl across the final two panels on the page, which got harder to read the more it went on – in every sense.

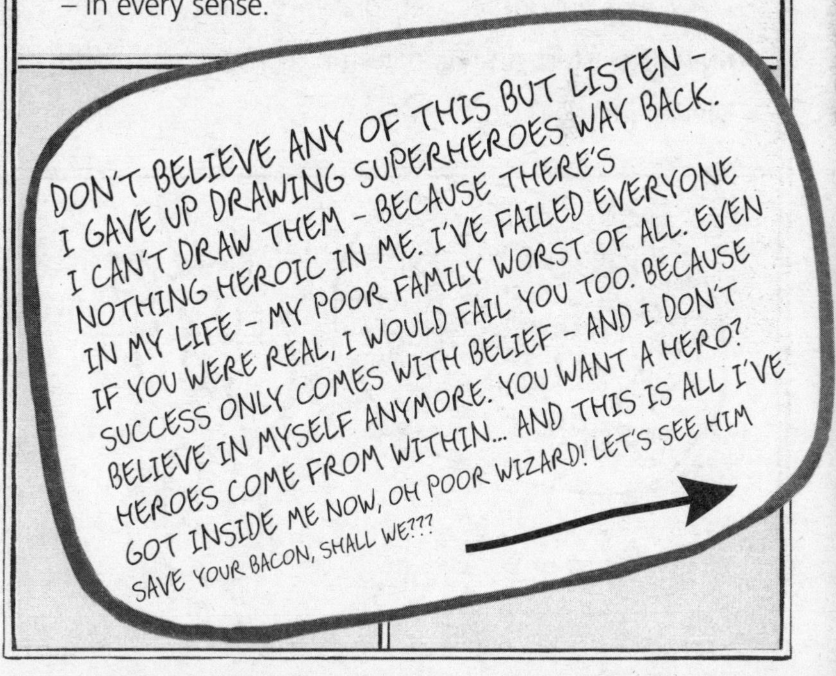

DON'T BELIEVE ANY OF THIS BUT LISTEN – I GAVE UP DRAWING SUPERHEROES WAY BACK. I CAN'T DRAW THEM – BECAUSE THERE'S NOTHING HEROIC IN ME. I'VE FAILED EVERYONE IN MY LIFE – MY POOR FAMILY WORST OF ALL. EVEN IF YOU WERE REAL, I WOULD FAIL YOU TOO. BECAUSE SUCCESS ONLY COMES WITH BELIEF – AND I DON'T BELIEVE IN MYSELF ANYMORE. YOU WANT A HERO? HEROES COME FROM WITHIN... AND THIS IS ALL I'VE GOT INSIDE ME NOW, OH POOR WIZARD! LET'S SEE HIM SAVE YOUR BACON, SHALL WE???

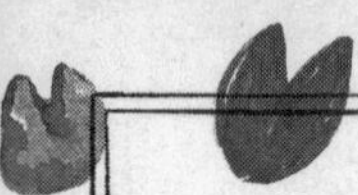

The harsh swipe of a quickly drawn arrow underlined the words, pointing off the page. I lowered the parchment, my eyes prickling with the promise of tears. I knew what that arrow had once pointed to.

What else? The picture of Posho Pig on the drawing board. My granddad's bitter joke.

But that wasn't the end of my discoveries. There was another sheet of talking parchment beneath. And my heart did a funny little jump.

A pretty hopeless drawing of a pig in a top hat sat in the first panel.

It could only have been drawn by Posho himself, trying to start the comic-strip conversation with Merlin, just as I had.

He sounded so hopeful and determined. But in the next panel, there was Merlin, clutching his head in despair. The entire third panel was a speech bubble :

GAHH! OH, GREAT GARRY PENDERS, HOW COULD YOU! I TRUSTED IN YOUR WORK AND YOU GAVE ME A PIG! THE MAGIC I USED IN HIS CREATION HAS LEFT ME ALL BUT SPENT – AND FOR WHAT? WHAT USE TO ME IS AN ARTLESS SWINE?

I couldn't help feeling that Merlin was the 'artless swine in all this – as the next panel saw the return of the badly-drawn pig; this time on his knees as if praying.

Obviously that had never happened; now I learned precisely why.

IN ORDER TO THWART THE THREATS THAT GUARD MY PRISON, I MADE THE MAGIC THAT MADE YOU TOO STRONG TO BE UNDONE – EVEN BY ME. YOU WILL LAST ETERNALLY, O USELESS, FOLLYSOME BEAST!

But Posho wasn't taking it lying down. He took it standing up with trotters on hips.

Hear me, sir! Though you spurn me and shun me, I shall not falter. I shall free you one day – never fear!

"Spoken like a true superhero," I murmured.

But Merlin had obviously been less impressed. Nothing had ever been drawn in reply.

Poor Posho.

So much fell into place at that moment – how Posho had come to know about Merlin's predicament. . . Why he'd seemed so jealous of my drawing talents. . .

Why the great Garry Penders had stopped drawing super-types walloping each other in order to focus on beating himself up. . .

And why Merlin had got so mad with Posho the other night. From the Big Man's point of view I could kind of see it – he'd gambled a whole chunk of his magical might in bringing my granddad's work to life, and in place of the hero he desired, he'd got a prank-playing pig. A prank-playing pig who wanted to be so much more. . .

The whole crazy situation seemed suddenly kinda tragic.

And, as I looked down at the floorboards, I saw there was something else lurking beyond the broken cobwebs of the cavity. Gingerly I reached in and felt the cold crackle of a plastic bag. Something soft was inside. Almost too afraid to look, I reached in. . .

And snatched my hand away at the sound of a scuffling behind me. I jumped, turned – and found Posho in the doorway.

"Hello, old boy. I've had to climb in through the landing window! Someone's put wood over. . ."

The pig saw me crouched over the floorboard and gasped. "Why, you. . . **Oink!** How dare you peek at my secret things! Put them back at once!"

"I'm sorry, Posho," I protested, stuffing the papers back into the hole. "I didn't mean to go through your stuff."

"**Oink!** You did!"

He had me there. "Well, yeah, all right, I did." I shrugged helplessly. "I just really wanted to know everything about this Merlin thing."

"Well. . ." Posho looked down at the floor, crestfallen. "Now, I suppose you do."

I nodded. "And what I know most is – you're amazing. The Big Man treated you so meanly, but you're still so loyal to him."

"Yes, well. . ." Posho sighed heartily and sank down on his haunches. "**Oink!** Merlin's magic brought me to life, so he must've placed the desire to help in my head." He held his head theatrically. "If only I could draw, I'd have got the Big Man out long ago! If only there was the faintest whiff of greatness or talent about me, I could've saved him with a clever plan. . ."

"Which reminds me why I came here – to a boarded-up attic." I looked at Posho and sighed. "Your clever plan with the bottles last night has kind of backfired. After meeting the neighbours, I think my mum and dad have gone crazy. . ."

I told Posho all about it. He did not take the news well.

"This is unthinkable!" He clapped a trotter to his forehead in theatrical despair. "Turning Posho's penthouse pad into some chintzy boudoir? Selling off my creator's belongings? **Oink!** It can't be true."

"It is," I said sullenly. "Mum and Dad are going to start clearing the place out today. So what are we going to do? How can we stop them?"

The pig considered. "We could arrange a little accident – you know, break your parents' arms or something?"

"What?" I frowned. "Are you crazy? We can't do that!"

"**Oink!**" Posho shrugged. "Very well. How about we only break their fingers? That'd still stop their vile decorating schemes."

"Back off from my parents!" I could hardly believe what I was hearing. "Anyway, how would that stop the guy who's coming to buy Granddad's drawing board?"

"We could clobber him on the back of the head with a sock full of coins," Posho suggested. "That'd sort him out."

"What are you, today, Psycho Pig?" I tutted. "No. What we need right now is for somebody to come to the rescue." I looked across to the drawing board. "A superhero or two we can ask for help."

"Or four," Posho agreed. "I'll fetch you the last of the parchment." He gave me a hard look. "Unless, of course, you've already found it?"

"Uh, no." I shrugged. "And I didn't look in your plastic bag, either."

"I should hope not! **Oink!**" He delved into the gap beneath the floorboards and pulled out some scrolls. "A pig's plastic bag is his castle, as the old saying… er, doesn't go. Here." He passed the parchment over. "This is all that's left, I'm afraid. Only three sheets."

"Which means three chances. . ." I listened hard,

but could hear no sounds from downstairs as I picked up the brush. Sparks seemed to spring through my fingers as I tightened my grip. "I'd better get going."

I'd spent so long staring at Merlin's heroes the night before that I could bring them to mind easily. The brush seemed to guide my hand even more than the last time, and the ink flowed as easily as blood from a wound – the kind of wound that War Commander might make as I drew his sword, gleaming in the light of some unseen sun.

It was such a thrill to see something I was drawing look so cool, so right; like something that belonged on the wall in this decades-old shrine to comic-book talents of times gone by.

"It's just a shame you'll never be as good as Stupendous Man," I murmured.

"Good work, old boy," Posho said. "Just think – all we need do is take this picture out into the moonlight and it will come to life! How I wish I could draw like that. . ."

Don't I know it, I thought with a pinprick of guilt.

After finishing off War Commander's slightly scary-looking armour, I decided to add a little flourish of my own – a big 'WC' on his chestplate. Yeah, I liked that, and I was sure this super-knight would get a kick out of it too.

"Water Closet?" Posho squealed. "But... that's an old fashioned word for a toilet."

"Shush!" I hissed. "It is not."

"It is!" Posho insisted, at lower volume. "Haven't you seen a WC sign anywhere before?"

Now the pig mentioned it, I had a suspicion I had. "Oh, great. I just invented Toilet Knight."

"Don't cross it out," Posho advised. "You'll make a mess of his armour. Anyway, he won't know. **Oink!** He's from a time without flush lavatories."

That was true, I thought. Besides, if Merlin and the moonlight did their thing as planned, Toilet Knight would only be around for an hour in any case.

With a sigh, I went straight on to have a go at Harvest Boy. His weird hairstyle... the eye-mask... his strong-but-scrawny physique and the magic sack on his back ready to receive ripe fruit and veg at a moment's notice, all were picked out on the parchment with precision as the brush and ink helped me to do my work.

Lantern Girl and Sonny Siege followed their fellow Magic, Inc. characters, but not quite as successfully. Was the magic beginning to fail or was I just getting tired? Whatever, I drew a still-quite-impressive Sonny Siege with his round head, crimson cape and a dead cow raised heroically over his head.

Well, kind of heroically. It's actually quite hard to look heroic when you're holding a dead cow.

Then an awful thought struck me. "If moonlight brings drawings to life, what about this dead cow? It might turn up as a zombie cow. That wouldn't be good."

Posho considered. "Add some stitches so it looks like a cuddly toy cow instead. What a wizard prank to play on Sonny Siege. He'll love it!"

"Hmm." I drew the suggested stitches, but now it just looked like Frankenstein's cow. I added a goofy smile to its face and drew some cotton wool stuffing coming out of its back. After all, a battered giant toy cow adds class to any superhero gathering.

But – uh-oh – with the problem cow taking up so much space on the parchment, I hadn't really left enough room for Lantern Girl. Chewing my lip nervously, I found myself doing her smaller than the others to fit the space. I couldn't get her face quite right at that scale, either. Her nose came out very big – well drawn, but **verrrrry** big. Still, the rest of her was about OK – and I made sure her hand was alight so she had her superpower, however rubbish it was.

"There," I muttered as I finished the inking job. "The not-very fantastic four."

"Poor Lantern Girl's a titch," Posho observed. "**Oink!** I'm sure she can still be useful, though. Perhaps she could light up the pit outside the Big Man's prison, the better to see the killer skeletons."

"Who will probably kill her in, like, two seconds." I put the finishing touches to her knee-length animal-skin boots. "There." A wave of tiredness struck me as I put down the brush on the board. Suddenly, I could hardly stand.

"Easy, old chap." Posho stuck out a porky arm to support me. "You've done well. Very well. Let's hope we have moonlight tonight. . ."

I surveyed the scene on the parchment. For a first go, it was pretty good, I decided. This was only a test-out, after all.

But how long did we have the drawing board for, before it was flogged to the collector?

"I should draw Merlin's mob again, before the decorating kicks off in here," I told Posho, peeling off the masking tape so I could pull the parchment from the table. "I really need to draw them better, so we'll have another set of superheroes in reserve if Mum and Dad really sell the drawing board tonight."

"That may be wise," Posho agreed, taking the parchment from me and passing me another sheet. "The Big Man said the heroes must be trained to fight as a team. **Oink!** I suppose that every time the moonlight re-creates these heroes, they will remember what happened to them the last time they were conjured into being, and learn from it."

"I. . . I'd better get straight on." I taped the fresh sheet to the board, but then had to close my eyes. I felt weirdly woozy all of a sudden.

"I think you should take a rest first, old bean," said Posho. "**Oink!** Your family will have finished their breakfast by now. Any one of them could come looking for you – and find all this."

He had a point. "OK." I pointed to my drawing. "Take that picture and hide it, yeah? And hide yourself too! Hopefully Mum and Dad won't start in here till after lunch. I'll be back up as soon as I can."

Posho nodded solemnly.

I left the attic and tried to tiptoe down the steps, but it came out as more of a flat-footed stagger. I was too tired to care. I lay down on my bed and almost instantly fell fast asleep.

I'd learned that drawing too much with magic ink takes it out of you.

But I hadn't yet learned quite *how much* it took. . .

CHAPETR TWENTY-ONE

A SHEDLOAD OF TROUBLE

It's like the old saying goes, "The best laid plans of mice, men and Stew often go awry." Because there I was, sleeping peacefully, when Mum suddenly burst into my room and announced she was taking me to town to get my new school uniform and to find a new leotard for Lib, who had somehow managed to lose her own.

Looking at my watch I saw I'd dozed for a couple of hours, but I still felt wiped out. "I. . . I thought you were vandalising the attic today?"

"Decorating, yes." She seemed much more her old self; I wasn't sure if that was good or not. "After lunch."

"And what about that guy who wants to buy Granddad's drawing board?"

"He's dropping by after dinner. Now, come on."

Mum pinched the bridge of her nose and shut her eyes. "Dear me, I've got such a headache!"

Well! She really WAS back to normal!

So out we went to the local boring shops, where I had to try on scratchy trousers and shirts, and tie an unfamiliar tie in a totally uncool way that Mum wouldn't moan about. I saw other boys my age out and about, and wondered if they went to my new school. I imagined trying to make friends with them, talking about normal, ordinary things in a normal, ordinary way. How could life ever feel normal again after this? I saw myself in the changing room mirror – and the boy in school uniform I saw there didn't feel like the real me at all.

Secret identities again.

Once we found stuff that fitted, I had to trail about with Lib while we found just the right shade of pukey pink for her new dance gear. I supposed it would go nicely with the attic's new paint job.

But it was my own paint job I was worrying about. I had the feeling that Disaster was looming. . .

Back home, after lunch, just as threatened, Mum

and Dad got started on redecorating. I couldn't understand why they were so determined to start today, when surely it made sense to wait until the collector guy had taken away the drawing board?

As it was, I had to help Dad shift it (along with the rest of the furniture) over towards the boarded-up windows before we hid the whole lot under dustsheets. Then Mum and Lib took down all the posters, pictures and certificates hanging on the walls and stacked them in my room.

Why weren't they going to show all that stuff to the collector? Surely he'd pay top dollar for them? It didn't seem to make sense – but I wasn't about to point that out to them. As you know, grown-ups are often weird and a bit stupid.

Now, I don't know if pink paint smells worse than any other kind, but I had to go outside to escape the stink. So I sat out in the back garden. It was a fair size and had brushes and shrubs and a few cool places to hide out which I'd always loved as a little kid.

And suddenly I realised it also had a shed. A shed with a window. A window through which you

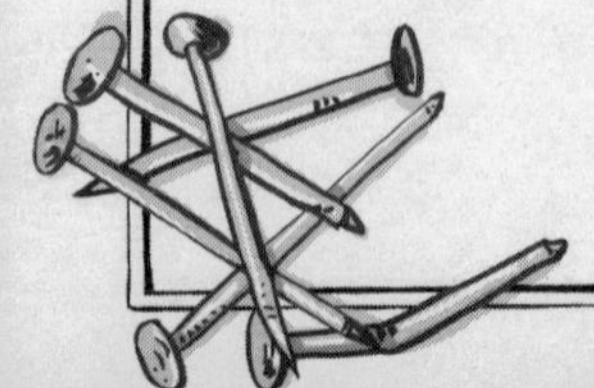

might see moonlight!

Hmm, I thought. With the attic out of bounds and superheroes to assemble, a shed with moonlit windows might just come in handy.

And clearly Posho had had the same idea, because just then he poked his head out of the shed door and beckoned me over. The shed was musty and damp and full of rusting garden tools. Its windows were swathed in dirty cobweb, and black tangles of papery legs twitched in every nook and cranny. Posho perched himself on a battered table already piled high with old-fashioned tins and boxes and bric-a-brac.

"This is a cool spot to bring Merlin's mob to life!" I hissed excitedly. "Mum and Dad won't hear all those heavy feet stomping overhead and if they look outside they'll only see the shed anyway! Why didn't you mention this place sooner?"

"It's my holiday accommodation," Posho said. "**Oink!** Though I dare say your pernicious parents will knock it down shortly, just for the fun of it."

I joined him in a gloomy sigh. "They've hidden Granddad's drawing board under old sheets and they're painting around it as we speak – so I can't bash out any more pictures of Merlin's fab four."

Posho looked thoughtful. "It's almost as if your mater and pater are doing everything they can to stop us. **Oink!** And if this collector takes the drawing board away tonight. . ."

"We're in trouble," I agreed.

"Don't forget, we still have this, old chap. . ." Posho raised his top hat to reveal the roll of 'living' parchment with my test pictures of Merlin's heroes. "**Oink!** We'll just have to keep everything crossed for moonlight tonight."

I kept everything crossed for the rest of that afternoon. It wasn't easy and it made me kind of sore.

But of course, I had to uncross several things so I could eat tea.

And maybe that's why my luck quickly ran out.

It was Lib's fault really. Out of the blue, as we were finishing off beefburgers and chips in the kitchen, Lib announced that she had drawn a 'Stew-eating monster' and that it would star in the first issue of her own comic called *Mega-Lib*, starring her as the superhero and me as the dweeby guy who needs saving. (AS IF!) The Stew-Eating Monster would start off as a picture in *'Comic Lady's Scary Comic'* and then, apparently, come to life to get me.

"That's nice, dear," said Mum.

"Since when did you like anything to do with comics?" I muttered. "Anyway, drawings coming to life? That's crazy!" I looked down at my plate, wondering if she'd been spying. "And even if it was true, I wouldn't need Mega-Lib to save me from Comic Lady – which is a rubbish baddie name, by the way – I'd just steal whatever she used to draw the Stew-eating monster and draw a Stew-eating-monster-eating monster to get rid of the Stew-eating monster."

"That wouldn't work," Lib retorted. "Because Comic Lady would draw a Stew-eating-monster-eating-monster-eating monster to eat your monster. So you would need Mega-Lib to save you."

"Mega-Lib couldn't save her own pants!" I said hotly, slapping down my knife and fork on the plate. "I'd just draw a Stew-eating-monster-eating-monster-eating-monster-eating monster to eat the Stew-eating-monster-eating-monster—"

"That's ENOUGH!" snapped Dad. "If you two have finished eating and can't think of anything nice to say, you can go to your rooms."

I was taken aback. It wasn't like Dad to get so grouchy so fast. "Uh… I was going to ask – can I use Granddad's drawing board one more time? Please?"

"Can I, too?" Lib chimed in.

I frowned at her. "No way! Since when did you care about it?"

Dad shook his head. "There's wet paint galore up there. I'll be getting the drawing board out soon – carefully – for the collector to see."

"Not fair!" I moaned.

"ROOMS, BOTH OF YOU!" Mum bellowed. **"NOW!"**

Banished again.

Me and Lib went out quickly and in silence. I thought Lib would start crying or something; she always did when she thought Mum hated her. But maybe, like me, she was just a bit too stunned.

Mum was usually more hardwearing than this; she'd gone into Atomic-Mother mode with very little pushing.

"That was your fault," said Lib.

I shot her a dark look. "Tell me, runt – where'd you get the idea of bringing comic characters to life, anyway?"

"I dreamed about it last night. Comic Lady was telling me about it."

I rolled my eyes. "I told you, that name is lame."

"Well, her secret identity's a really good name." Lib stuck out her chin. "It's Vivian with an E. Viviane."

"Viv. . . Viv. . . Viviane?" My throat contracted. My mouth went dry. My eyes went a little bit crossed.

"Yes, Viviane." Lib frowned. "I don't know how I know there's an E on the end, but there is. Cool, isn't it?"

"Icy," I muttered.

Could it really be coincidence that Lib had dreamed about the evil enchantress who had locked Merlin away in his prison-tomb? A dream where drawings came to life?

A chill went down my spine. Then it went back up my spine, wiggled in and out of my shoulder-blades, took a detour around my collar-bone and went back down my spine again before zipping through my bottom and turning my guts to ice-water. It was quite a chill. It would probably have won multiple awards at the World's Chilliest Chill Contest.

I gripped Lib by the shoulders. "Are you sure Comic Lady's name was Viviane? This is important. Tell me more about the dream. What did Comic Lady say? Was the Stew-eating monster her idea? Did she say anything about a wizard—?"

"Stop acting so weird, Stew." Lib scowled and pulled away. "You'll only get us into more trouble."

"I think I might have done that already!" I began. "See..."

But Lib had slammed the door and I was left alone on the landing.

Alone and suddenly afraid, my brain crowding with questions.

Had Viviane got a whiff of Merlin's escape plan?

Was she onto me?

Was she planning something to stop us?

Had she been responsible for Mum and Dad's suspiciously all-of-a-sudden desire to board up and redecorate the attic, trying to separate me from the drawing board and the power of moonlight on the magic ink?

Had she somehow messed with their minds to make them extra-cranky so they grounded me in my room – separating me from the board even further?

Was this collector guy coming round to get the board so quickly because Viviane had told him to?

Was he actually NOT the real collector but a freaky supernatural demon in human disguise?

Was he going to try to kill me in some horrible fashion?

Was I ever going to stop asking myself scary questions to which I didn't really want to know the answers in any case?

You're acting crazy, I told myself.

Yeah, right, myself told I back. 'Cos everything else lately has been completely un-crazy and normal – right, Stew? You're doomed! You mess with magic, this is what you get! You wanted to become king of the comics the easy way like a big cheat, and now you're going to suffer!

If this were a movie, at that precise point you'd have seen the camera closing on my face, tilting to one side as I clutch my head in my hands and shout: ***"NOOOOOOOOOOOOOOOOOOOOOOOOOOOOOOOOOOOOOOOOOOOOOOOOOOOOOOOOOOOOOOOOOOOOOOOOOOOOOOOOOOOOOOOOOOOOOOOOOOOOOOOOOOOOOOOOOOOOOOOOOOOOOOOOOOOOOOOOOOOOOOO!!!"***

But this wasn't a movie.

It was real. And I was in real trouble.

So I clutched my head in my hands anyway and shouted,

"NOOOOOOOOOOOOOOOOOOOOOOOOOOOOOOOOOOOOOOOOOOOOOOOOOOOOOOOOOOOOOOOOOOOOOOOOOOOOOOOOOOOOOOOOOOOOOOOOOOOOOOOOOOOOOOOOOOOOOOOOOOOOOOOOOOOOOOOOOOOOOOOO!!!"

CHAPTER TWENTY-TWO

HEROES ASSEMBLE!

(No jokey misspellings now – things are getting serious)

I ran into my room, closed the door and pressed my back against it, trying not to shake. I had to warn Posho we could both be in danger. But since I couldn't risk sneaking downstairs past Mum and Dad to get outside, I'd just have to climb out through the window, Posho style. No problem – so long as I didn't lose my grip on the drainpipe and the ivy and plunge to my death ten metres below.

It was nippy outside. Night was slowly falling as I sprinted for the shed.

Posho could tell immediately that something was wrong, big-time – mainly because, as I burst in, I cried, "Posho – something's wrong, big-time!"

I spilled the beans about what had happened in the house and Lib's freaky dream.

"So," said Posho softly. "Viviane is reaching out

to us through time just as Merlin has. **Oink!** But we can't let her stop us."

"Right. Perhaps you should spring the old bucket-of-water-above-the-door trick on her," I said with just a little sarcasm. "That'll put an end to her evil schemes."

"Do you really think so?" said Posho.

"Nope." I sighed. "Oh Posho, I'm scared. I never imagined we'd have to face a supervillain ourselves. Do you think she's coming to kill us so we can't save Merlin? Do you think she's killed him already for trying to escape?"

Posho gulped. "There's only one way to find out if the Big Man's still alive. . ." He peered out of the shed window to where a faint moon shone through dark tissue-paper clouds. "If we wave our parchment under a spot of moonlight, his magic ink will bring four superheroes leaping to life – and we'll send them back through time to see. **Oink!**"

He took off his topper and I snatched the parchment from inside. "Do you have the Spell of Time Transportation too, or whatever it is?"

Posho pulled a piece of crumpled parchment from inside his jacket and placed it on the corner of the table. "Here it is."

"Then I guess we're good to go." I unrolled the picture and placed it on the desk in the measly moonlight, holding down the corners with old tools and bits of junk.

Within moments, the magic started to happen.

My stomach tied itself in knots as I watched the ink-strokes on the parchment begin to darken and smoulder. Tiny coils of smoke were rising up from the bold lines to make four three-dimensional forms. Sparks fired and crackled in the haze, as if tiny invisible beings had started a gunfight inside these smoky creatures.

"Bless my piggy little soul! **Oink! Oink!**" Posho clasped his trotters to his chest, standing beside me. "Here they come!"

And there I went, backing away into a pile of garden tools that fell with a clang and a clatter. At the sound, the smoky shapes stiffened and grew more defined. I could see the shine of armour through the mist around the tallest figure. . .

Welcome, War Commander!

The humped shoulder of the scrawny thing beside him was looking more like a sack; yeah, a magic sack...

That one had to be Harvest Boy...

And surely that was Sonny Siege beside him, misty muscles hardening, a ghostly cow held high above his head... While the glow that now lit the shed like a bare lightbulb could only be coming from the flame-like fingers of Lantern Girl, who was...

Actually she looked kind of short compared to the others. Ooops.

In another blink, the four figures became flesh – and the cow that Sonny Siege was holding became a stuffed toy, just as I'd intended.

My mouth dropped open. My eyes were on stalks.

I forgot my fear, watching these impossible, magical creations stare back at me and Posho. They looked like actors in amazing costumes, cast for their uncanny resemblance to the original heroes. Well, except for Lantern Girl, who was *really* short and did have one heck of a nose. But three out of four wasn't bad.

And I helped to make you, I thought, wonderingly. I helped to make magic. It was a moving moment, actually. It felt—

"What place of poop-stinking devilment is this?" boomed War Commander in a deep, gruff voice. Lifting the visor on his helmet to reveal his swarthy face, he noticed his fellow super-types. "And who are you weirdos?"

"Oi!" Harvest Boy swept his sack off his shoulder and frowned up at the knight, baring Bugs Bunny teeth. "Who are you calling a weirdo?"

"I'm calling the lady dwarf with the mighty nose and the round-headed guy cuddling a stuffed cow weirdos." War Commander gave a lofty smile. "*You* I'm calling a turnip-smelling weirdo. Got a problem with that?"

Harvest Boy narrowed his eyes. "You'll be the one with the problem, when I poke a parsnip up your bum!"

"**Oink!**" Posho murmured. "They're not getting on, Stew, just as you predicted."

But they've got to, I thought. Because suddenly I'd had a brainwave.

"Posho," I breathed. "If War Commander and the others could somehow get the drawing board out of the attic and out of danger, I'd be able to make more superheroes. . . some can act as our bodyguards while the others set Merlin free!"

"Capital idea, old chap!" Posho snuffled enthusiastically. "And rescuing a board shouldn't unduly challenge four superheroes."

"In theory," I agreed.

But from the look of things, Sonny Siege's very existence was challenging him. He kept looking down at himself and then up at the stuffed cow with the bad stitching as if trying to remember where he'd found it. Lantern Girl, meanwhile, had pushed between Harvest Boy and War Commander and pointed her glowing finger up at War Commander's chest.

"You rude knight!" she snapped. "Your words are as filthy as the water closet whose name you bear!"

"Eh?" War Commander stared down at his breastplate. "Hey, who drew 'WC' on my armour?"

"How do they know about toilet stuff?" I hissed.

"You must've drawn them with that knowledge," Posho hissed back. "**Oink!** Quickly now, address them, old sport! Get them on our side!"

"Hey!" Sonny Siege spoke at last, puzzlement on his face as he studied the cow in his hands. "This beast isn't plague-ridden at all. It's a stuffed toy! I'll never lower the morale of a trapped, half-starving community by throwing a stuffed toy over a wall. . ."

War Commander smirked. "Why not throw the dumpy damsel here over a wall instead? She'd lower anyone's morale."

"How dare you!" squealed Lantern Girl.

"Aha!" Sonny Siege's eyes lit up as he spotted Posho. "Yonder pig looks like he carries a disease or two."

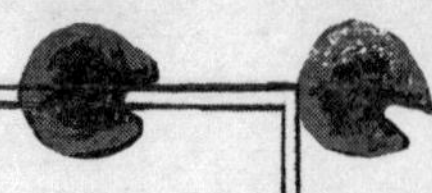

"You wrong me, sir!" Posho blustered. "I'm a pig in my prime."

"Um, excuse me, everyone," I broke in nervously.

War Commander glared at me, raising his sword. "Who are you, boy? How came we to be here?"

"I'm S-S-S-Stew Penders, sir!" I stammered. "I drew you all in Merlin's magic ink and the moonlight brought you to life. The Big Man needs you to rescue him! And the woman who's got him locked up is up to something here too!"

Four blank stares were turned on me.

"Ah." Posho looked awkward. "I seem to recall a time of some confusion at first. It took me a while to remember I was actually a comics character with no real prior existence. **Oink!** And it took longer still to feel bothered about the Big Man's plight. . ."

"Now you tell me!" I groaned, before facing my creations and trying again. "Look, you guys are superheroes, right? I've drawn you, but you were made up originally by a wizard called Merlin; it's his magic ink that's brought you to life. Look at the picture on the table behind you. . ."

But Harvest Boy had started sniffing the air. "I don't know what madness is going on in this place, but I smell crops nearby. Crops to be gathered!" He turned and smashed open the shed door. "That means I am needed, and so I must away!"

"No, wait!" I hissed, starting after him. "You can't go, I need you here!"

"I can detect horses in this neighbourhood." Sonny Siege was smiling happily. "Oooh, I could just do with throwing a horse." He sped away after Harvest Boy.

"Come back!" I watched helplessly as two of my heroes escaped into the gathering night. "You can't just go! Merlin said that the ink's magic will wear out. In an hour you won't even exist!"

"Enough of your prattling, boy," War Commander declared, lowering his visor. "It is time I went a-questing – for a smith or an armourer who can remove these shameful letters from my breastplate!"

"Huh?" I shook my head. "No, you're in the future, War Commander, a different century – there's no one like that round here." I grabbed the parchment from the table. "This is where you're from – ink and imagination! Please, try and remember. . ."

But War Commander was already striding out of the shed – and Lantern Girl was right behind him, bashing him on his armoured bottom as she went. "Don't think I'm finished with you, Toilet Knight. . .!"

I turned to Posho. "She may not be finished, but we are. This is a super-sized superheroic catastrophe. What are we going to do?!"

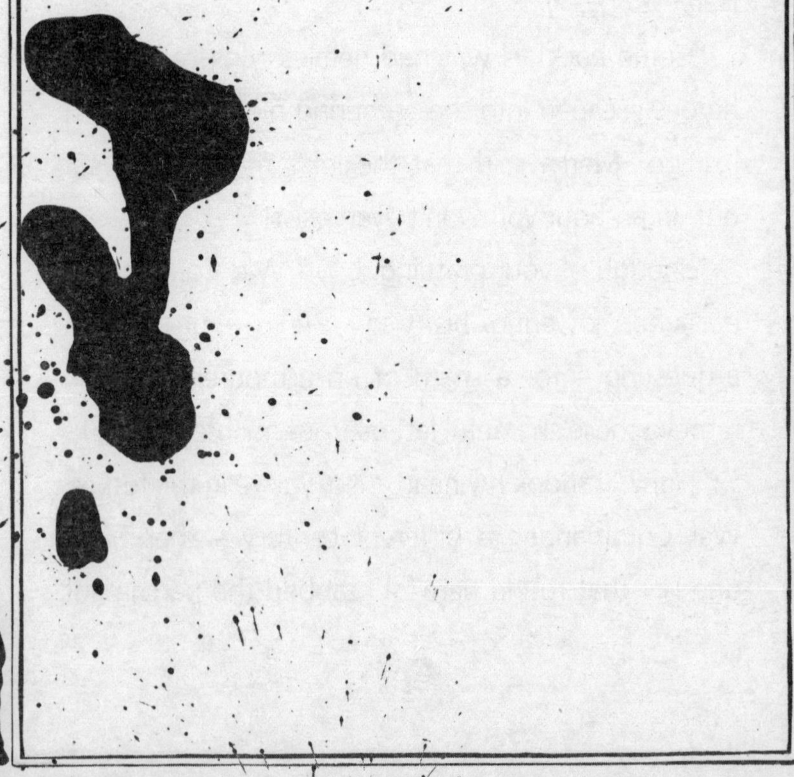

CHAPTER TWENTY-FREE

FROM BAD TO WORSE

"Come on," I said decisively. "We've got to get those super-loopers back and force them to understand the situation." I dragged Posho with me towards one of the tangled paths, where we could hopefully leave the garden for the front of the house unseen. "If Mum and Dad see them, they'll flip out and call the police!"

Posho was looking pale. "Harvest Boy has super-speed, remember – we'll never catch him up. As for Sonny Siege—"

"He must've smelled the stables up the road." I shook my head helplessly.

But as I reached the garden gate and scrambled over, it seemed that things were only going to get worse. There was no sign of War Commander, but at the end of the front drive I saw Lantern Girl kicking a lamppost, a look of fury on her face.

"Trying to outshine me, huh?" she was snarling. "I don't know what you are, tall stone thing, but I'm going to flatten you!"

I shook my head. "So she knows about toilets but not about street lights?"

"We were talking about toilets as you drew the pictures, remember, old fruit? **Oink!** We never mentioned streetlights—" Suddenly Posho was interrupted by a car alarm and a loud metallic **SCRUNCH**.

My heart sank. "Uh-oh. Guess we never mentioned cars, either!"

Hurrying to the end of our drive I saw that War Commander had decided to battle a silver Mercedes parked just up the road – he'd hacked open its bonnet and now its hazard lights were flashing orange, its siren wailing at ear-splitting volume. "What manner of beast are you?" WC cried, swiping the Mercedes again with his sword. "Hold your unnatural tongue!"

Distracted from the lamppost, Lantern Girl looked over at the rumpus and scowled at the flashing

hazards. "Does everything make light in this terrible place?" She ran over to the car and started kicking and punching one of the Merc's front tyres. "Go dark, metal beast! Mine is the power of light! Mine alone!"

"Get away from there!" I yelled, already aware that curtains were twitching at the neighbours' windows; if I ran over, I'd be seen for sure. "Quickly – there's someone in trouble back here! Someone who really needs a superhero!"

War Commander and Lantern Girl both turned and ran towards me and Posho, while Posho and I darted back through the gate into the back garden, even as I heard front doors opening along the street. Luckily the car alarm was drowning out any noise we made now – and would draw Mum and Dad's attention to the front of the house, not the back.

"Well, boy, what is it?" War Commander demanded. "I understand not this unnatural world, and my sword yearns to taste the blood of a powerful foe."

Lantern Girl, stood beside him, raised her glowing fist. "And I shall never stand by while an innocent soul is in danger!"

"Great!" I nodded enthusiastically. "Because I need you to rescue a table."

They stared at me.

"A table," WC echoed without enthusiasm.

"Come on, you've got to remember." I held up my original drawing of them all. "This is where you came from – Magic, Inc.'s magic ink! Merlin, the Big Man, created all of you, and gave me the power to bring you to life just by drawing you."

"The wizard," War Commander murmured. "You know, I think I do remember him. . . My creator. . ." He nodded slowly. "And somehow, I know. . . Merlin needs us."

"Right," I agreed. I guessed the ink-link was getting across some of Merlin's desperation and despair to these characters, just as it had with Posho – providing magical motivation for their struggles ahead. "If we're going to save the Big Man, we need to get the special drawing board out of that attic there," I insisted, as Posho obligingly pointed a trotter towards the boarded-up attic window.

"I. . . I think I remember too." Lantern Girl looked

indignant. "But you drew us, yes? So, it's down to you that I'm the size I am? You didn't like my normal height, I suppose? You didn't like my nose?"

"I'm very sorry," I told her through gritted teeth, "this was only meant to be a practice run. . ."

Then the car alarm clicked off and the harrowing wail of a neighbour echoed eerily into the night. "My caaaaar... Look at my beautiful caaaaaar. . .!"

"Hark! A soul in distress!" War Commander raised his sword. "To the rescue!"

"NO!" I grabbed hold of his sword arm. "You're the one who *caused* the distress! Look, I'll draw you better next time, Lantern Girl, OK? But for now, please. . .?"

"Very well," War Commander boomed. "Come, small one. You must light my way while I search for this sacred table we are to rescue." So saying, he picked up Lantern Girl and hurled her towards the window. Stifling a scream, she just managed to catch hold of the sill – and held on there, huffing and cursing. With a hearty chuckle, the great armoured WC climbed heroically up the ivy to join her.

He prised off the boarding and clambered inside, and Lantern Girl quickly followed.

"Well done, old chap." Posho took and shook my hand. "First rate superhero management."

"Right. It's all going great," I agreed. "Apart from the totally trashed car outside. Not to mention the heartbroken neighbour, and. . ."

I trailed off as a sudden whistling noise filled the air, and glimpsed something massive hurtling groundward. **THUMPCH!** An enormous impact beside me knocked me off my feet. I fell onto Posho, he fell to the ground and both of us stared in bewildered amazement at the sight of Sonny Siege, the Living Trebuchet, beaming down at us with a terrified Shetland pony clamped under each of his muscular arms.

I groaned. ". . . and definitely not to mention the stolen horses!"

"Behold!" said Sonny Siege happily, "these hapless mares from the strange stables suffer from a shrinking sickness! When tossed over a castle wall their disease will surely spread and reduce the enemies of mighty Arthur to the size of fleas!"

"Let them go, you medieval muppet!" I hissed, trying not to lose it. "The only thing wrong with those horses is that they're being suffocated by your armpits!"

"Remember the big man of magic, old boy!" Posho piped up. "Remember your comic-strip creator? He needs you!"

Sonny Siege's eyes clouded over. "My creator. . . needs me. . .?"

But the next moment there came another whistling noise from the sky – and a pumpkin broke open on Sonny's head. He dropped the Shetland ponies, and they reared up and bolted for somewhere saner as more vegetables rained down from the sky – turnips and parsnips and marrows and potatoes. . . I wished I was riding one of them to freedom. The ponies, I mean. Not the potatoes. "Now what?" I wailed.

"I've just found the harvest to beat all harvests!" cheered Harvest Boy, whizzing down from the sky to land beside Sonny Siege, his magic sack stuffed to overflowing. "What an age this must be. Vegetables!

Fruits! Strange boxes and exotic bottles and jars, all growing together in curious bunches in an impossible walled garden of glass and brick. . ."

"The supermarket in town, you mean?" I couldn't believe what I was hearing. "You *stole* all this stuff?"

"I gathered it!" said Harvest Boy defensively. "That's what I do."

"You nicked it! What kind of a superhero are you?" I cried, dodging as one of the panicked Shetland ponies galloped past again. "Think about Merlin! Your creator! You've got to save him! How can you do that with half a supermarket in your sack?"

"Half? Nay, lad, I don't do things by halves!" Harvest Boy proudly began to upend his magic bag. "I gathered everything!" A humongous jumble of stuff came tumbling out – carrots and strawberries and coffee and bottles of liquid soap and an actual cash till. . .

"Stop it!" I ran over and shoved Harvest Boy in the chest; with a yelp, he overbalanced and fell down beneath his own magic sack. "Posho, what can we do? This has all gone completely pear-shaped."

"And very nice pears they are too," Sonny Siege observed, studying some of the fallen fruit closely – then throwing it miles into the air.

Posho pulled on my sleeve. "Look, old boy! **Oink!** The attic window!"

I looked up and saw War Commander waving cheerily. "We found the table!" he called. "But alas, I fear it will not fit through this window. Can I chop it up a bit?"

"Keep your voice down!" I hissed; Mum and Dad – or even Lib, for that matter – would surely be on their way to see what all the noise was. I couldn't believe they weren't here already. And what would they find when they looked out? Twenty tons of shoplifted goods, a couple of stray horses, the house-breaking pig in a top hat, a compulsive thing-thrower with most of a pumpkin on his head and. . . a knight trying to jam Granddad's drawing board through the window.

"Forsooth," the knight cried, "the task is a challenging one. . ."

I stared up at the precious desk.

And then, with a chill, I realised there were drawings on the living parchment I'd taped there; pictures of a monster that was part shark, part crocodile, one of which had been clumsily crossed out. Both creatures shared a speech bubble; squinting through my glasses I made out words brushed in childish writing: *Stew... Stew... Yummy Yum!*

I froze. The breath felt punched from my lungs. The artwork was good but the writing was wobbly like a six-year-old's, like. . .

"Oh, Lib," I breathed. "What did you do?"

My sister had said she'd drawn a Stew-eating monster. She just hadn't mentioned she'd drawn it on the magic parchment, at the board, with Merlin's brush, in magic ink.

Ink that was now steaming in the moonlight, as grotesque, monstrous shapes began to twitch and shimmer into life. . .

SPECIAL SUPER-SIZED CHAPETR TWENTY-FOUR

CARNAGE IN THE GARDEN OF DOOM!

Posho jumped in the air in alarm. "War Commander, quickly," he oinked, "take the table out of the moonlight!"

"Light?" Mishearing, Lantern Girl scrambled up onto WC's shoulders at the window, waving her glowing hand. "Who wants some light? Here you go!"

"NOOO!" I yelled. "The picture, it's bad, get it away—"

But by now, War Commander had seen the sparkling mist-shapes and was reacting in typical style. "Wraiths of evil – **TASTE MY STEEL!**" he thundered, and with sword in hand took an almighty swing at the ghostly shapes. The blade swept through them harmlessly – and then bit deep into the drawing board.

With a splintering crunch, the drawing board, and the parchment, split in two.

"**NOOOOOOO!**" I yelled again, more loudly, as both halves of the precious drawing board plummeted to the ground, trailing the magical sparkling smoke like exhaust.

And I realised that Posho was already galloping towards the bits of the board. To my astonishment, he stuffed one half of the steaming parchment into his mouth and then hurled himself on top of the other pic.

"Posho!" I ran over to join him, Harvest Boy and Sonny Siege close on my heels; however bonkers they might've been, they were still superheroes. War Commander and Lantern Girl scrabbled swiftly down from the window to join us. Posho was looking sick and sweaty.

War Commander was puzzled. "Where are yon wraiths?"

Lantern Girl preened herself. "My light scared them away!"

"More likely your nose scared them away," said WC.

"Be silent," said the diminutive damsel, "before I pass water in your armour as your name invites."

"Shush!" I hissed. "It was Posho who stopped the monsters. How are you feeling, Posho?"

"**Oink**," the pig said feebly. "Had. . . to stop moonlight. . . reaching your sister's picture. . . couldn't sit on both. . ."

"But you ate it while it was coming to life," I hissed.

"I panicked!" Posho admitted. "And I should warn you, I'm ready to panic again at any moment!"

I couldn't blame him – his stomach was making ominous rumblings and there was a green sheen to his usually pink skin.

"The swine is most unwell," said Sonny Siege cheerily. "My, what a weapon he would make, if I threw him over a—"

"Will you stop going on about chucking sick animals around? We need to destroy that picture he's sat on before. . ." I trailed off as a wisp of sparkling mist escaped Posho's mouth. "Uh-oh."

Suddenly, with a belch that sounded like drains unblocking, Posho swelled up like some terrible balloon, becoming five or six times his usual size until he towered above me. I jumped as a huge fin burst through the back of his overstretched jacket, and his top hat went flying as his head inflated and his snout grew longer, greener, bristling with teeth.

"Lo!" War Commander stared at the creature formerly known as Posho. "Yon pig has become a sinister beast!"

I didn't need an overgrown tin of beefsteak to tell me what had happened. Posho had eaten the magic ink while it was coming to life, and now it was concluding the process inside him – changing him with it, just like Bruce Banner changing into the Hulk!

Only there was nothing superheroic about this transformation. I could've cried with fear as the curly tail grew broad and scaly, as the neat little trotters turned to talons at the end of huge arms and legs, as the mischievous eyes turned red and narrowed. . .

"Posho's turned into a Stew-eating monster!" I yelled, staring round at my gaggle of superheroes in a panic. Suddenly the beast lurched towards me, jaws opening wide to bite me in two. I jumped backwards. "Help!"

"I'll not let this hell-hound make a stew of my harvest," Harvest Boy declared, grabbing his huge sack of stolen goods. "Whole villages may starve! I must hide it somewhere."

"With the lives of countless villagers at stake, I shall light the way for you!" Lantern Girl declared, and they both charged away toward the woodland at the back of the garden. "WC and the Trebuchet will hold off this beast till the foodstuffs are safe."

"Not that kind of stew!" I shouted. "*I'm* Stew – the only thing it wants to eat is ME. Viviane's tricked my sister, I know it. This is part of her plan to stop us freeing Merlin. Come back!"

"Have no fear, boy," boomed War Commander. "I shall slay this vile beast for you."

Will you? I thought. Time was ticking by – how much had passed already? But even as I fretted, another monster burst into being behind War Commander, knocking him to the ground with a sweep of its claws. This beast had a face that was horribly mangled – where Lib had tried to cross out her drawing, I guess – and that seemed to make it angrier. It lurched towards War Commander and its mashed-up jaws bit into his armoured leg.

"Arrrgh!" WC's shin guard crumpled like an old tin can. He swung his sword at the hideous creature, but missed – it had already spat him out and turned towards me, its sticky nostrils twitching with the succulent scent of fresh Stewart Penders.

"Eat. . . Stew. . ." it rasped. "YUM."

The Posho-monster beside it (from now on to be known as the 'Ponster', if that's OK with you?) joined in, though more haltingly. "Stew. . . eat. . .?" It took a few hesitant steps in my direction.

"They're after the boy!" cried Sonny Siege.

"Yeah, noticed, thanks!" I turned to him as I went on backing away. "If you fancy throwing that thing a mile into the air, don't let me stop you…"

"Of course!" The Living Trebuchet stepped boldly forward and tried to grip the Ponster round the middle. It didn't protest – almost as if Posho was resisting its evil urges, somewhere inside.

But while the Ponster didn't object, the scribbled-out Stew-eater did. Its jaws opened wide and it sucked Sonny Siege inside like a superheroic strand of spaghetti. With a yelp, he was snatched from sight, tumbling down the monster's gullet.

"No!" I yelled helplessly, shocked and horrified.

All right, so Sonny wasn't really real, and would've vanished anyway in another forty minutes or so. But to see him get gulped down by an impossible monster. . .

"Trebuchet, you shall be avenged." War Commander stood bravely in front of me, his sword raised. "This means WAR!" He started hacking away at the Scribbled-Out Stew-eating monster (from now on to be known as the SOS-monster, as it's catchier. Clear?), but the disgusting creature hardly seemed to notice.

Cowering behind WC, I tore at my hair. "If Merlin's right, it'll only be here an hour," I told myself. "If we can just hold if off till then. . ." I groaned. "But the heroes were made first, they'll vanish sooner! Oh, if only Harvest Boy and Lantern Girl hadn't gone. I *knew* Merlin's lot would be useless!"

Then, in a rush, I remembered my silly argument with Lib from earlier, and how I'd go about defeating Comic Lady's bad guys: "I'd draw a Stew-eating-monster-eating-monster to eat your Stew-eating monster. . ."

"Toilet Knight!" I cried. "I mean – War Commander! Up in the attic when you found the table, did you see a bottle of ink and a brush and any more sheets of parchment?"

"No time to write a will, boy," cried WC. "I need assistance."

"Assistance with the monster?"

"No, with my hessian underpants. They're really starting to chafe." He glanced back at me, eyes murderous. "*Yes,* assistance with the monster, you young oaf!"

"Hang in there," I told him, "I'll be back!"

Bunching my fists, I ran towards the back door. But what if I led the monsters into the house? I felt a brain-mangling sense of guilt for all I'd been doing in secret – Mum, Dad and Lib, they were all in danger. I had to warn them, quickly, get them. . .

"OUT!" I shouted, bursting into the living room where Mum and Dad were sitting in front of the TV. "Get out, quick, there are monsters and they're going to eat me and maybe trash the house and. . ."

But Mum and Dad didn't react. They didn't even look my way. They just kept staring and smiling at the telly. It was wrong, all wrong.

Magic, again, I thought with cold certainty. Viviane had done something to them. Stopped them interfering. Taken them out of the picture.

And speaking of pictures – the only thing I could do was start drawing. But had Lib left the parchment, brush and ink at the drawing board in the attic, or taken it somewhere else? As I got up the stairs I could hear her snoring in her bedroom.

"Lib! The stuff you drew with, where is it?" I burst into her room, clapping my hands, then jumped up and down on her bed. She didn't stir. "Come on, Mega-Lib is supposed to save me from Stew-eating monsters, remember?" I scooped up some of her toys and chucked them at her. "Lib, I'm pulling the heads off all your mermaids and ponies – you'd better wake up!"

It was no good. Not so much as an eyelid flickered. How could she be sleeping so deeply?

I could guess the answer. Starts with V, ends in E. And I'm not talking about **v**il**e** **v**ic**e**-president **V**aleri**e** the **v**ol**e** with a **v**as**e** in a **v**alis**e**.

Viviane was using my own sister to stop me helping Merlin.

Feeling sick and scared and angry, I charged up to the paint-stinking, sheet-strewn attic and hunted about for the ink and the brush and the all-important parchment. But WC and Lantern Dwarf had left the place in a total tip. Outside I could hear the *thwack* of sword on monster-hide and another growl of "Stew, lovely Stew. . ."

It sounded even closer now.

Finally I found the pot of magic ink, lying on its side, the precious indigo dripping away through the floorboards. I grabbed the jar – it was all but empty.

And there was the brush – sticking out of a tray of pink emulsion.

"Noooooo!" I groaned, whipping it out and wiping it on a dustsheet. After drawing her pics, Lib must've used the brush to 'help' Mum and Dad with their evil decorating – and she'd daubed a fair amount over the remaining parchment too, bright pink doodles and splashes. It was ruined!

If my heart had sunk any further it would've been squelching out through the sole of my foot. But I jammed the brush into the dregs of the inkpot, and clutched the ruined parchment to my chest. And that was when the Ponster appeared at the attic window, its hideous face staring in at me.

I felt rooted to the spot with fear. . . But to my amazement, the Ponster winked at me.

"Posho," I breathed. "The *real* Posho, I mean – my friend. You're still in there, aren't you?"

The Ponster nodded urgently and bowed its head – and I saw that it had reared up to stand at the window, offering itself as a kind of horrible ladder to speed my journey down.

"Whatever your plan, boy, hurry!" bellowed War Commander. I could see the SOS-monster gazing about for me crossly. The remains of the drawing board were just a few metres away from its crocodilian claws. . . I was petrified!

But I had no choice.

I scrambled out through the window onto the Ponster's hard, green back and gasped as he suddenly dropped back down to earth. The jolt of landing threw me clear – but I landed right beside a bit of drawing board and hit the ground inking.

The space left on the parchment was a funny, skinny shape – but as I drew, I decided that the Stew-eating-monster-eating monster had balloon-like skin that would stretch wide as he swallowed his food, the same way that an anaconda would eat a rabbit whole and it would sit like a big lump in its snaky body.

Frantically I drew my monster with fierce eyes on stalks and rows of flesh-chomping teeth and powerful legs to give it more agility than the SOS-monster. It was uncanny how good it looked, even drawn at something like four-fifths the speed of light.

"Here's where your plans come back to bite you on your Dark Age bum, Viviane!" I cried.

But the SOS-monster had seen me. Its eyes, already narrowed to burning slits by the scribbles scored over its face, nearly shut all together as it sniffed the air and growled: **"STEWWWWWW..."**

Flattening War Commander into the ground with its powerful tail, the SOS-monster prepared to charge.

"Posho?" I called desperately, "hold him off!"

As I drew big, muscular arms on my creation, the Ponster stumbled towards his evil, scribble-faced twin – and was instantly thrown aside. I held up the parchment to the glowing moon like an offering.

The SOS-monster slithered towards me.

The pink-splashed parchment began to steam. . .

And suddenly the SOS-monster was running straight into the jaws of a real-life monster-eating monster!

I backed up against the wall, watching in fright and wonder. My big, wiggly creation was red as a boil and vicious as a viper, just as I'd pictured it in my mind. The SOS-monster turned aside at the last moment, trying to escape. But my monster was not to be denied. He bit down hard on his desperate dinner, crunching through the crocodile hide, the enormous fin sticking in his teeth.

The SOS-monster gave a despairing roar as if it already knew it was beaten. But, in one final act of spite, it lunged for the remains of the drawing board with its mangled chops. . .

"No!" I yelled.

Too late.

CHAPTER TWENTY-FIVE

R.I.P. THE END

All the yelling and crying in the world couldn't change it: the SOS-monster had gulped and guzzled down every last splinter of Granddad's drawing board, and most of the paint-splattered parchment with it. It snuffled hungrily for the brush and ink as well. . .

But it was too slow. My Stew-eating-monster-eating monster, in just a handful of breathtaking, blood-chilling bites, devoured the SOS-monster completely.

Silence fell across my back-garden battlefield. The only noise was the thump of my pulse, the jangle of my half-shredded nerves – and the squeak of War Commander's armour.

"By the fiery heavens. . ." The silver knight pushed himself up on his elbows, mud, blood and exhaustion all over his face, and groaned at my monster.

"Not another beast to battle?"

"No, it's all right." I helped him to stand. "This one's on our side." Although, that said, I didn't like the way my monster was eyeing the Ponster, who lay puffing for breath on the churned-up lawn. "Go and hide yourself in the bushes," I told the thing. He shrugged and shuffled off, obligingly shielding himself from sight.

"What now?" asked War Commander.

I was about to say what a good question that was, when footfalls alerted us to the ragged return of Harvest Boy and Lantern Girl.

"Look out!" the potato-loving boy wonder yelled, pointing at the Ponster.

"It's all right," I told him. "I think the real Posho's still in there. He was brought to life from a drawing in the same way, I think that must be helping him keep control. . ."

A humungous belch burst from the Ponster's gruesome jaws.

"Mostly," I added.

"Ugh!" Harvest Boy choked, and War Commander

closed his face visor. "That whiff would wither a field of wheat! We were doubly wise to shift the harvest!"

Lantern Girl nodded, holding her enormous nose with glowing thumb and finger. "I lit up a clearing in the forest. . ."

"Then I buried everything, out of sight." Harvest Boy beamed, his face red and bright with sweat. "Even the funny metal things with coins inside!"

"Terrific," I sighed, wondering what the police or future archaeologists would make of that.

"While you dug a hole, we were *left* in a hole." War Commander glared at them. "You should've heeded the boy – is he not the messenger of our creator? While you tarried, the Living Trebuchet was eaten!"

"And so was the drawing board," I said despondently. "Which means, even if I had loads of ink and parchment, which I don't – I can't draw you again and make you better. Viviane's done well." Looking at each of them in turn I took a deep, deep breath. "So guess what? You three are the Big Man's only hope. If I can send you back into the past, to your own time. . . do you think you can you set your creator free?"

The three superheroes looked at each other. To be honest, they made a sorry sight.

And I was sorriest of all. It seemed my first fumbled attempt at drawing Merlin's characters was to be my last. But would the three heroes still standing (just) be enough to save the Big Man? The magic would wear off in a half-hour or so – would that be enough?

"We're not exactly in peak condition," said little Lantern Girl at last, "But we'll give it a try."

"Aye," her men-friends agreed.

"We owe the master our existence," War Commander added. "We must aid him now."

"Great!" My heart quickened with sudden nerves, and I hurried to the shed on wobbly legs. "I. . . I'll get the 'Spell of Time Transportation'. Hang on. . ."

I grabbed the pieces of parchment from inside the shed – and with a queasy twinge, I saw that my drawing of Sonny Siege had disappeared from the group portrait, leaving only a burned and blackened shadow. As I took the parchment outside to study it more closely, the breeze blew the shadow away. A ragged cut-out was all that was left. I swallowed hard. If the heroes die in the real world, they vanish from the parchment too, I realised.

Shivering, I decided not to show the others. Time was running out and their job was hard enough already. Thirty minutes left to save the greatest wizard in the world from the toughest prison in the world created by the baddest wizardess in the world. . .

Maybe they could do it. Maybe they'd be all right.

"Are you ready?" I asked.

My superheroes nodded. The Ponster's guts rumbled ominously again.

"Make it quick," said Lantern Girl.

So I read the spell aloud:

Heroes mighty, disappear
Take thy butts away from here!
O'er the seas of time now sail
To set the Big Man free –

Don't Fail.

I didn't think it was much of a spell, to be honest. But at once, a mystical glow enveloped the trio, bombarding their bodies with bursts of brilliance. They began to fade from sight. War Commander raised his sword to me. Harvest Boy swung his magic sack over his back, and Lantern Girl looked crossly at the flecks of light as they outshone her glowing hand, which was growing fainter like the rest of her. . . like WC. . . like Harvest Boy. . .

The glow quickly faded, leaving silence. A silence broken only by the Ponster with a high-pitched fart.

"I hope you're not stuck like this for ever, Posho." I sighed. "Go and hide with the Stew-eating-monster-eating monster. He shouldn't try to eat you, but. . ." I gasped as the stench reached my nostrils. "But if he does, flip knows you've got a good defence mechanism." I went into the house to check on Mum and Dad. It wasn't good – they were still sitting there like zombies in front of the telly. Lib's snoring carried downstairs from her bedroom. Before I could get properly depressed, the doorbell rang.

I almost jumped a mile.

Quickly, I folded the two sheets of parchment and stuffed them up my shirt. Viviane wasn't locked up and weak like Merlin. She was strong enough to get inside my family's heads. Who knew what else she could get up to?

It took all my courage to call through the front door, "Hello?"

"Hello. I'm John Barnard, the collector," came a deep, puzzled-sounding voice. "And. . . I have no idea what I'm doing here."

"You don't?" Warily I opened the door. It wasn't an obvious witch-sent demon standing on the doorstep – it was a chubby man, scratching his bald head. "Let me guess, was it something to do with a drawing board?"

"Hmm. That sounds familiar. . . Something to do with. . ." Mr Barnard clicked his fingers. "Garry Penders!"

"Well, I'm afraid – very afraid, as it happens – that the drawing board has. . . gone. Stolen, kind of thing. Chopped up into firewood, in fact. And then the firewood. . . also stolen. Kind of thing." I cleared my throat. "Basically, no drawing board."

"Seems I've had a wasted journey." Mr Barnard shrugged and smiled at me. "Oh, well. I don't know why I took off in such a hurry anyway! Wasn't feeling myself at all. . ."

I could've explained, of course –

I SUSPECT, MR BARNARD, THAT AN EVIL ENCHANTRESS FROM DARK AGE TIMES PLACED AN URGE IN YOUR MIND TO TAKE AWAY THIS VERY IMPORTANT, SECRETLY MAGICAL DRAWING BOARD. NOW THAT IT'S BEEN DESTROYED, SHE NO LONGER NEEDS YOU.

BUT WHY DIDN'T THE ENCHANTRESS JUST MAKE YOUR PARENTS TAKE THE DRAWING BOARD DOWN THE TIP OR SOMETHING?

JUST AS A HYPNOTIST CAN'T MAKE SOMEONE PERFORM AN ACT THEY WOULD NEVER NORMALLY DO, VIVIANE COULDN'T FORCE MY PARENTS TO DUMP THE BOARD AS THEY'RE FAR TOO GREEDY. . .

ACTUALLY, SOME HYPNOTISTS ARGUE THAT THEORY IS NOT TRUE. . .

SORRY, MR B, I'D LIKE TO GET ON WITH THE STORY NOW.

Anyway, like I said, I could have told Mr Barnard why he wasn't feeling himself – except I could suddenly feel MYself. My stomach in particular, which seemed to be on fire. . . "Bye!" I gasped, slamming the door

and whipping out the parchment from under my top. It was burning, blackening. With horror I saw the pictures I'd made of War Commander, Harvest Boy and little Lantern Girl going up in smoke.

PFFFT! WC fizzled away to nothing.

POP! Lantern Girl was gone in a spasm of sparks.

HISSS! Harvest Boy's sack spilled cinders, the ink-work blazing bright until — **WHOOSH!**— the parchment blew apart in a black explosion of comic-strip confetti.

"No," I said hoarsely, as ash fell from the parchment like tiny black petals. It left a gaping space in the form of four former superheroes.

I thought of the way War Commander had fought on so valiantly against the monsters. . . poor little big-nosed Lantern Girl with her feeble hand-power. . . bumpkin-brained Harvest Boy missing the point of just about everything, and poor Sonny Siege, eaten alive. Well, as alive as any of them had ever been. They were things of magic, just passing through. But I had helped to make them, and for the brief time they had been here, they were as real as anything else in my crazy life. Except now. . .

"They couldn't get the Big Man out," I breathed. "They're dead. It didn't work."

"What didn't work, Stew?" Mum was standing in the living room doorway, rubbing her head. "Are you all right? What's been going on?"

Dad was just behind her, looking puzzled. "I think we must've dozed off or something."

"Hey! Who's been chucking my toys around?" called Lib from upstairs.

"You know, it's really odd," said Mum. "I can hardly remember a thing about today."

I wished I could say the same. But my throat was tightening; I just ran to Mum and Dad and held them tight.

CHAPTER TWENTY-SIX

NO, YOU CAN'T BE SERIOUS! NOOOO! etc

I was a bit of a mess as I sat alone in my room, later that night. Well, a lot of a mess, really.

Now back to normal, Mum and Dad were concerned about the shell-shocked vibe I was giving off and sat me down for a chat. They thought it was stuff to do with the house move, and having to start at a new school with no mates and other stuff like that.

I didn't bother to disagree, though in fact, I'd pretty much forgotten all that real world stuff. It felt like nothing in comparison.

It's funny, I remember Granddad often told me that superhero comics were really important because their stories dished out so many big emotions. By viewing heavy stuff through the eyes of a superhero, you understand it better when it happens to you – or so he said.

Well, my comic-book escapades had left me feeling all kinds of things for real that night, none of them very nice.

I felt **outrage** at how Viviane had messed with my family's heads.

FEAR that she would mess with them again – or come after me.

Sadness that Merlin would now surely die in his terrible prison, if he wasn't dead already.

Bitterness that all my star comic-book illustrator dreams had just dribbled away like the magic ink.

ANGER at myself for feeling more bitterness than guilt.

And a whole mixed-up bag of stuff about Posho.

I'd broken away from Mum and Dad's worried embrace earlier, saying I wanted a bit of fresh air in the garden. Luckily they didn't go out and notice what a state it had been left in, churned up by giant monsters and terrified ponies and various supermarket items. I found the brush and the empty magic inkpot and put them in my pockets. But there was no chance of anyone finding the monster and the Ponster in the bushes because both had disappeared; the hour was up and the magic had dissolved.

Posho had gone.

Later, as I lay on my bed with the brush and the inkpot, I felt really flat. I'd only known that pig for a few crazy days but already I missed him. Even his silly pranks. And there was no one else I could talk to about any of this. No one who could possibly understand. . .

I looked at the pictures from the attic stacked in my room. At the front was a framed photo of Granddad, drawing at a table, with Grandma beside him, both of them smiling, taken before stuff went bad between them.

"We can choose to be the heroes of our own stories, Stew. There's always a choice." Granddad had told me that so many times I was word perfect. *"When you see the way a superhero behaves, it helps to show you the right thing to do. You can take a bit of their courage and, in your own small way, be a superhero too."*

Now, of course, I realised what he'd really been saying: *"I couldn't find the courage when it counted,*

Stew. Make braver choices than mine."

"I tried, Granddad," I murmured, putting the ink and brush on my bedside table. "In the end, I think Posho had more guts than either of us. . ."

Something suddenly occurred to me. My pictures of Merlin's band of brothers (and their short sister) had gone up in smoke when they ceased to exist. Now Posho had passed on as well, had Granddad's portrait of Posho burned away beneath the attic floorboards too?

It would be just my luck if some magic embers burned the whole house down or something. Better check it out, I thought, grabbing my torch.

Luckily, Mum and Dad had gone pretty much straight to bed, worn out as Viviane's spell wore off. And Lib was sleeping properly now, muttering in her sleep about picnics and unicorns.

The attic was still a mess; I supposed I'd better clear it up a bit before Mum and Dad came back up here in the morning. The drawing board was gone of course – how to explain that? Then I remembered pretty much an entire supermarket had been emptied in bizarre circumstances, and no one would ever know how or why. Like Posho's breaking bottles from nowhere, the fate of the disappearing drawing board would remain a mystery. . . to everyone but me.

Quietly I eased up the floorboard and pulled out the scrolls and papers. As I did so, I heard the crackling crumple of the plastic bag hidden in the cavity's darkest depths.

I hesitated. I knew it was private, but then. . .

Quickly, I reached into the bag, flinched as my fingers closed on something soft and cold. Slowly I pulled out whatever lay inside. . .

And found myself holding a purple leotard. Lib's missing leotard! The neckline at the back had been stitched clumsily to a cape made from a purple towel. Daubed on the front of the leotard in black marker pen was the letter P in a big, wobbly circle. A pair of old tights – the ones Mum hadn't been able to find – had been cut down and sewn over the leotard's leg-holes.

I knew what I was staring at. It was a superhero costume. A rubbish, homemade superhero costume. . .

Made by – and for – a pig.

"Posho wanted to be a hero," I murmured. "And in the end, he really was. He gave his life in the hope that—".

Hang on a second.

There were no ashes at all in the cavity. I checked through the papers – and my heart felt like a bouncy ball, hurled into my ribcage.

The portrait of Posho was still there. It hadn't burned away!

Did it mean. . . ? Could it mean. . . ?

I didn't dare believe it. Maybe the portrait hadn't burned because it was twenty years old and made with more potent magic than my own drawings.

Maybe that was it.

Quietly, I replaced the floorboard, took the parchment and the costume back down to my room. . .

And almost screamed at the sight of a creepy figure standing by the open window beneath a ghostly sheet.

A very familiar voice went **WOOO**

I saw some very solid trotters poking out from beneath the sheet. "No way– I mean, it can't be– I don't believe– You can't be… POSHO?!"

"In the living, breathing, pink-and-naked-'cos-I-lost-all-my-clothes-when-I-mutated-into-a-monster flesh!" Posho whipped away the sheet, did a brief nude can-can on my mattress, then leaped into my arms, snuffling and snorting and trying to hug me. I couldn't keep my balance, dropped all I was holding, tripped over a box of comics – and then we both fell heavily onto the floor, nearly smashing into the stack of Granddad's pictures.

We held our breath for a few seconds, hoping Mum and Dad hadn't heard and woken up. When there was only silence we filled it with giggles of relief at a happy reunion.

"You're not just alive, you're back to normal," I gushed. "How? Where have you been?"

"I suppose that when the magic hour passed, the monster part of me passed too," said Posho thoughtfully. "**Oink!** And it was so awfully painful, I'm afraid I passed out, in the bushes."

"It's so good to see you," I said. "I'll even forgive you for trying to scare me with that rubbish ghost prank."

"I told you, I can't help my nature." A familiar crestfallen look crept over his face. "**Oink!** If I could, I'd be a superhero who saved the day, like War Commander and Harvest Boy and Sonny Siege and Lantern Girl and—"

I shook my head forlornly.

"They..." Posho swallowed hard. "They didn't save the day?"

I brought Posho up to speed on all that had happened. "It's not fair. It's terrible!" Posho pouted, resting his snout on his trotters. "Oh, if only I could be a superhero! If only I was good enough..." He shivered. "If only it wasn't so nippy in the nuddy."

"I, er... have something you could wear." Kind of awkwardly, I picked up his little costume. "See? You *can* be a superhero."

"You shouldn't have found out about that, Stewart!" Posho turned puce. "That's private. I mean... **Oink!** I made it for a joke. A silly wheeze, that's all..."

"No, you didn't." I held it out to him. "I saw your conversation with Merlin. You've always wanted to be a superhero – really, really badly. Haven't you?"

"Well..." Posho nuzzled against his costume like a baby with a blanket. "Yes. I've wanted nothing more since the moment I was made. **Oink!** But I know it's absurd."

"It's not. Don't forget, it was Merlin's magic that brought you to life but Granddad who drew you." I looked again at Merlin's sad exchange on the talking parchment with the late, great Garry Penders. "He stopped drawing superheroes, but I don't think he ever stopped believing in them – even if he stopped believing in himself. He told himself he was no good because of how he'd behaved in the past… just like you're telling yourself now. Maybe he passed those mixed-up feelings on to you through the magic ink, somehow?"

"**Oink!**" Posho dropped his costume and looked up at me with watery eyes. "Do you mean to say that's why I'm longing to be a superhero, though I know I'm not good enough?"

"Don't say that!" My voice came out fiercer than I'd intended. "Deep down you know what you were put here to do. You've dreamed of being a superhero your whole life. So have I. That's something Granddad's given us both, in different ways."

Posho half-smiled. "The belief that we can be the heroes in our own stories?"

"That's it exactly," I agreed. "Belief. Belief. . ." I could almost taste the word in my mouth. . .

And then the flavour suddenly turned sour.

"Oh, man," I murmured. "Posho, I. . . I never really believed that Merlin's superheroes were up to the job, did I?"

Posho considered. "You displayed a certain lack of enthusiasm, yes."

"What if I accidentally passed that lack-of-enthusiasm onto War Commander, Harvest Boy and the others through the magic ink, just as I passed on the idea of a WC?" I sighed. "What if, because I didn't believe in them when I drew them, they came out kind of. . . half-hearted?"

"**Oink!** You think that's why they didn't fight so well and were beaten so quickly?" Posho gave a wondering whistle. "Heavens to Betsy! Great Scott!"

"Lousy Stew, more like!" I felt like crawling under the bed and staying there for ever. I was about to put my head in my hands—

When I saw something on my thumb and finger. The old magic ink stain. It was back. Faintly, very faintly. Only this time, it seemed twisted into strange spindly shapes... almost like...

Letters?

ALL NOT LOST

"Look, Posho!" I beamed, my heart doing yet another impression, this time one of a jumpy, bumpy thing steered by an insane mouse. "Merlin's still alive! He's got to be – all's not lost! See?"

Posho blinked, and pointed to my hand. "The ink's shifting!"

PIG SHED
PAPER BOARD
PIC

"What the hecking flip does that mean?" I whispered, squinting at the already near-invisible ink.

"That I'm only fit for a pig shed!" Posho's eyes started to well up with tears. "With the last of his power, the Big Man confirms his hatred for me. **Oink!**"

"No crying," I warned him sternly, "your mega-

tears will wash the ink away. Come on now, think – what does 'paper board pic' mean?"

"A picture drawn on paper on a board?" Posho wiped his snout and shrugged. "We don't have a board any more – or any paper."

"Merlin must be working his magic pretty hard to communicate like this. He wouldn't bother telling us what we already know." I looked around the room. "Think, think, think. . . " Then I noticed a tiny smudge of ink on the picture of Granddad at the table with Grandma. Pages of art were scattered over it. Granddad's ink and brush were sticking out of a small drawer under the tabletop—

"Posho!" I grabbed him by the pork belly and he nearly squealed. "That table – it looks just like the table in the shed you were sitting on."

"By Jove!" Posho peered more closely. "It's a lot older now and somewhat mouldier but yes, it could be that very item of furniture."

"And if we read the words on my hand from top to bottom instead of across, it says 'Pig Paper' and 'Shed Board Pic'." My excitement was growing. "In that pic, you can see Granddad's been illustrating. Maybe that table's what he used for his work before he got the drawing board!"

Posho dared to smile as he got what I was driving at. "Meaning some of the old master-artist's magic could be lingering around that tabletop. But we don't have any living parchment—"

"Pig paper!" I held up the portrait of Posho drawn by Granddad all those years ago. "There's a little bit of room at the side there, look."

"But that parchment's secondhand," Posho argued. "The moonlight's already touched it, twenty years ago. And besides, we have no ink."

"All's not lost, remember? Merlin said so! There's got to be a chance. . ." I scrambled over to my bedside table and checked the inkpot. There really was next to nothing left. "Arrgh! No way is there enough for four characters." I looked at Posho. "But there may be enough for two small, pretty basic drawings."

"**Oink!** Which of the Big Man's heroes would you choose?"

"None of them," I said. "After what happened

before, I wouldn't take the chance. Instead. . . " I picked up his raggedy costume and pushed it into his trotters. "I'd choose the two heroes I really believe in. Stupendous Man. . . and you."

Posho's voice shrank to the size of a cat-flea's earlobe. "Me?"

"You ate Lib's Stew-eating monster picture while it was coming to life and it transformed you," I said, trying not to tremble. "So if I draw a picture of us in superhero mode which we show to the moonlight and then swallow it down. . ."

"We turn into superheroes for an hour?" Posho gulped. "**Oink!**"

"I know it's not the greatest origin story in the world, but it's all we've got to work with." I checked the calm silver of the moon through the window, and that strange sense of destiny came over me again. "Tonight, I reckon fate's giving us one last chance to show the Big Man – and ourselves – that we have what it takes to be real heroes. And to show Granddad, wherever he is, that he didn't do so badly, passing on his dreams to us."

Slowly, very slowly, Posho smiled. "Just imagine if we did manage to save the Big Man's life. . . **Oink!**" He soon grew grave again. "But of course, any hopes for success are dependent on a foolproof plan."

"Not only foolproof, but dragon-proof, skeleton-warrior-proof, siren-proof, rock-proof and who-knows-whatever-else-proof." I took hold of the brush, which tingled faintly in my hand. "So, come on, Super-Posho, let's head to the shed – and get plotting!"

CHAPETR 2-SEVEN

DO OR DIE

(OR CRY, LOUDLY)

That very night, while Mum and Dad slept and snored, and while Lib dreamed peacefully of all the dumb things she loves so much, I was outside with a pig in a superhero costume, gathering together all the items we thought we might need if we were to stand the teenie-weeniest chance of staying alive during the crazy, terrifying ordeal that surely lay ahead of us – or rather, over fifteen hundred years behind us in a dark land of myth and monsters which could only be reached through the last flecks of magic ink and a spell from a wizard who had to be on his last legs. . . or more likely his last toes. . . or even his last toenails. . .

To say I was scared is an understatement. And I knew too that I was in over my head. In fact, I couldn't even see my head anymore. Hang on, where the flip was my head? Hello? Head?

Posho and I – keeping our heads – had planned and plotted and were gathering stuff in case Merlin's magic couldn't bring our superhero alter-egos to life with the pulse-poundingly powerful powers we needed. We might well be left with no powers at all – aside from the power to poo ourselves in terror at incredible speed – and so taking along some bits and bobs that might possibly help us stay alive for a few seconds longer couldn't hurt.

Luckily, Harvest Boy had buried the contents of an entire supermarket in the woods at the end of the garden, and the police had not yet thought to look there – so our options were wider than they might ordinarily have been. I know technically that was stealing, but I excused it with the knowledge that if we actually did the job and made it back home, we could replace whatever we'd taken with the vast riches Merlin would heap upon us as a reward for saving him.

Yes, I'm afraid it's true; the thought of owning my own comic company with myself as star artist was still splashing about in the backwaters of my head. The thought of it had kept me swimming stubbornly against the tide of my every instinct to run away and hide under the bed.

Actually, while Posho worked on some last-minute preparations of his own, I did go back inside the house. I just wanted to look in on Mum and Dad, and Lib, to say a little goodbye.

You know. In case I never saw them again.

Because aside from the risk of death by mythical monster, I knew there was a chance that Merlin might be so weak by now that he'd run out of magical puff before he'd taken us all the way back to 500 AD. Which, while it would mean we'd be spared a hideous battle, would also mean I'd be stranded with Posho in the distant past. We'd turn back to our normal selves when the hour was up, but the Spell of Time Transportation was a one-way trip; I could end up as a Victorian street urchin or a Tudor beggar or a medieval peasant. And whatever the year, Posho could end up as someone's roast dinner.

Then again, perhaps things might work out even worse. . .

What if I accidentally infected the ancient world with modern germs, against which old-time people had no defence? I might destroy the human race and all established history. I guess Posho would argue that would leave things looking up for farm animals, but even so. . .

"Sweet dreams," I whispered to Lib. "I guess mermaids and ponies and stuff are as important to you as comics are to me. So. . . enjoy them, OK?"

Then I opened Mum and Dad's door. But my throat felt tight again, too tight for me to say anything at all, so I waved kind of pointlessly, trudged downstairs again and went back outside.

The garden was still and silent (though I thought I caught the occasional anguished sob from the house of the man with the mashed up Mercedes as he filled out an insurance form). The moon was shining brightly.

The shed door jumped open as Posho pushed his head out, still clad in his not-all-that-super superhero costume. "Well, Stewart old boy, our provisions and equipment are all bagged up and I've cleared a space on the old drawing table. . ."

I looked past him at a glistening mountain of bulging black plastic. Batman had a utility belt – we would have to make do with twenty-two numbered utility bin-bags.

I crossed to the shed, and as I entered, Posho pulled a brand-new-from-the-cleared-out-supermarket beanie hat down over his head. His ears stuck out through slits in the top, and his eyes gleamed through two crudely-cut holes. He'd added a pair of pants and an extra 'P' to his costume.

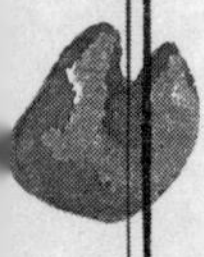

"Nice name," I said approvingly. The portrait of Posho with its precious blank spaces was taped to the wooden table top. The narrow space on the parchment shone ghostly white in the moonbeams. The brush and the hardening ink stood in the half-open desk drawer.

"Well, old chap. . . I'm ready if you are." Posho smiled bravely. "And I think you should only draw Stupendous Man. Not me."

I stared at him. "What?"

"We both know the Big Man's magic is on the

wane. **Oink!** I've had more than my fair share already. I've weakened him enough." Posho blinked out solemnly through his eyeholes. "I insist you save his strength so he can give the maximum to you."

"But—"

"I mean it. I don't want any more help." There was a steelier edge to Posho's voice now, as he pulled up his tights. "I need to know that being me was enough after all. Do you understand?"

I smiled at him. **"Oink,"** I said.

He bowed his head graciously. "In your own time, then."

"And into Merlin's, with any luck," I agreed.

Whether that luck would be good or bad, we'd soon find out.

I picked up the slender brush and started to draw.

Sharp crackles leapt through the veins on my arms. "Hey! The arty vibes from this old desk are stronger than the ones at the drawing board!" I gasped as my hand jerked the brush in small, superfine strokes. "They're really taking charge!"

"Your grandfather was a young man starting out on his career when he drew there." Posho's eyes were glinting with excitement. "Full of energy and passion for pen and paper. . . just like you!"

"Just like me," I echoed, my resolve hardening like the threads of precious ink embroidering the old paper. I was drawing myself as Stupendous Man and it really did look stupendous, the best ever. And already those smoking hot lines were starting to smoke for real. . .

"It's happening!" squealed Posho. "Down the hatch, old bean! Quickly!"

Hands trembling, I tore my drawing from the paper, trails of magical smoke tickling my fingers, sparkling in my eyes – and, before my courage could fail me, I stuffed it in my mouth. The taste of must and magic fizzed on my tongue, heated my throat, then sent thousands of volts sparking and jumping through my internal organs, zapping and fwapping and thunderclapping inside me, swelling my muscles, strengthening my spine, beefing me up, up and away as I. . . I. . .

How can I describe what it was like to be transformed – after years and years of dreaming and longing – into an actual superhero?

It felt like I was changing into someone bigger, faster, stronger and better than me – and yet I was still the old me inside. Muscles rippled under my skintight costume. Potential pulsed in every cell. For all I knew, I had veins full of ink now, but. . . wow. It sure did feel good.

I should've been scared but I wasn't. It was as if all the geeky games I was supposed to have grown out of had somehow mingled with the dreams

I was supposed to have put away, and made me. . .

Well, they'd made ordinary Stew into something stupendous.

"Awesome," I whispered; to my surprise, my voice was the same; too young and high for my now-manly frame.

Posho, though, remained pleasingly impressed. "Right-ho, Stupendous Man – **Oink!** – you've got an hour, tops – and counting."

"I'd better grab our stuff," I said, trying to make my voice lower and tougher to match the rest of me. Bounding away to the pile of numbered bin bags, my cape catching in the breeze, I felt my heart spin giddily in my new, super-enhanced ribcage at the ease with which I lifted our haul – a dozen bags clamped in each huge fist.

"Good work, Stupendous Man," said Posho. "But the real test is – do you have your absorbing abilities?"

I felt the smooth, glossy texture of the bin bags in my hands... then flicked one finger at a nearby rose bush. There was a shimmer of air like a heat haze in the moonlight, and the bush became a crumpling heap of black PVC. **"OMG!"** I stared at my fists and fingers. "It works! I did it!"

"Capital, old boy!" Posho hurried to stand close beside me. "**Oink!** But don't zap me with your incredible, real-life superhero powers!"

We looked at each other and then we started to giggle and snort with gleeful laughter.

"Now, we'd better not waste time or any more magic." Posho cleared his throat. "Are you ready for me to recite the Spell of Time Transportation?"

"Ready and steady," I said. "Go."

Posho read the rhyme aloud in his most dramatic 'Power Pig' voice:

Heroes mighty, disappear
Take our butts away from here!
O'er the seas of time we'll sail
To set the Big Man free –
All Hail!

And then fireworks began to bang and crack inside me. The world around – the garden, Granddad's house, the shed, the sky – all began to dissolve. Me and Posho were slipping away. Centuries began to blow and bluster around us, harder, faster, colder, freezing me through my suit. . .

SM

Then suddenly the journey was over. Like stepping off an invisible escalator, Posho – sorry, Power Pig— and me stumbled forward into a white, wet, misty world. I dropped the bin bags with a rustling clatter and a brimstone stink caught hard in my nostrils.

"Is this the right place?" My voice sounded small and had no echo. "The right time?"

"It's er. . . a little hard to tell, old bean." Posho pulled up his leotard and peered through the curling mist. "Any sign of a great dragon with fiery breath and poisonous claws?"

I stepped forward, fear hardening in my chest now while wet pebbles crunched mushily under foot. Cliffs loomed up through the smog like an avenue of chalk skyscrapers, creating a kind of natural arena.

Arena? As in fighting? Fighting to the death against. . .

A shrieking roar, high and hate-filled, slammed through our bones. I dropped the utility bin bags. The terrifying howl seemed to swallow the air around us. And I realised the mist was not mist at all.

It was smoke.

Smoke that was breezing from the horrific, hanging-open jaws of a gigantic reptilian beast. A craggy, coal-black behemoth, its scaly skin like shining rock hacked from the heat-mines of hell.

"Ah," said Posho quietly. "That must be the great dragon."

Doesn't look so great to me, I wanted to wisecrack, superhero-style; but I couldn't mumble the slightest reply, as the dragon's lava-red eyes opened like bullet-wounds, and its black teeth bared in a welcoming grin.

Welcoming us to our deaths. . .

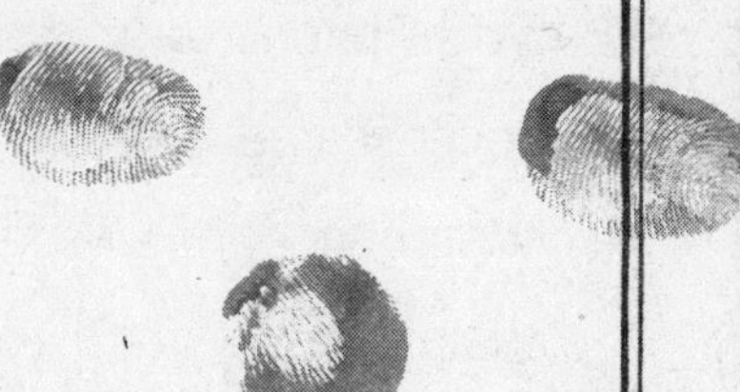

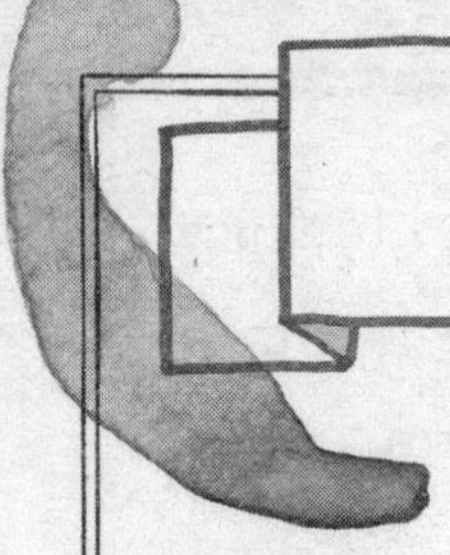

CHAPTER TWENTY-ATE

TIME'S A-DRAGGIN'

The dragon's shadow swamped me like a suffocating blanket.

Unless you've ever stared up at a giant dragon rising to its full and awful height, extending its rock-sharp poisonous claws towards you as its jaws hiss and steam with a growing, glowing fireball that you just know will be spat your way at any second, you might find it hard to appreciate just how mega-ultra-super-scared I was at that exact moment – even in superhero-form. Especially since I was also aware that I was a good (or rather, very, very bad) one-thousand-five-hundred years away from everything and everyone I knew and loved and my only friend and ally was a prank-playing cartoon pig currently wearing my sister's leotard, my mum's tights, an unidentified pair of pants and a beanie hat.

Luckily, it was this very pig who saved my bacon by reminding me we had actually prepared for this encounter.

"Utility bin bag three, old bean!" yelled Posho, his trotters a blur as he sprinted through the smelly fog to where I'd dropped the PVC bundles. "Coming your way!"

He threw the bag towards me – but it fell hopelessly short.

Luckily for me.

I scrambled over to try and catch the bin liner. And moments later I felt a blistering heat on my back, as crimson flames engulfed the very spot where I'd been standing. Yes, Stupendous Man very nearly had the shortest career of any superhero in the world.

As it is, I didn't die. I just fell to my knocking knees and pulled out the contents of the black sack. . .

A netted bag of lemons.

The perfect anti-dragon defence – when you're Stupendous Man.

With another blast of stinking, smoking air, the

dragon reared up and raised one huge, rocky paw to splat me. But I wasn't having it. I jumped clear, the mighty muscles in my legs heaving me high into the air so that I landed on a ledge some way up the nearest cliff face.

Below me, with a jolt, I saw three blackened silhouettes had been burnt into the chalky rock. One bulky and big, one scrawny and one way too small.

So this was what had become of them – War Commander, Harvest Boy and Lantern Girl – Merlin's Rescue Mission version one, the poor things, fallen at the first hurdle. Dead and burnt down to their shadows.

As I turned back to the dragon, my fingers curled into fists. No way was Stupendous Man about to go the same way.

I squeezed the lemons tight. In my stories, Stupendous Man could absorb the properties of anything he touched – and, sure enough, I felt the sharp tang of the fruit entering the fingers of my left hand. Moments later, a blast of pure citric acid burst from my right palm – and it was the very best feeling in the world. Every time I'd drawn Stupendous Man in the act of absorption, I'd always wondered how it would actually work to have that power, and now I knew.

It was an absolute rush.

"Top hole, old boy!" Posho yelled, cowering among the bin bags, "but don't forget to aim it at the dragon!"

The dark, jagged monster, its skin aglow like hot coals under bellows, was reaching out to carve me from the cliff face. I sent the supernatural spray of essential lemon-ness right up into the creature's face, stinging its sizzling eyes, drenching its deadly maw. It recoiled, steam blasting from its body with a noise like hissing boa constrictors, shaking and shuddering.

"Keep it up!" Posho urged me.

But then something like a huge dark girder accelerated out of the smoke towards me – the tail of the dragon. I hurled myself aside as the snaking weapon pulverised the cliff face, spraying it as I went somersaulting through the air in a hail of boulders. But as I fell, I lost hold of the lemons.

Posho squealed and buried himself for cover as debris fell in a hard rain all about, and I landed on my back in the middle of the bin bags. There was foul-smelling smoke everywhere, I couldn't see where the dragon had gone, nor what state he was in, and without the lemons. . .

"Here!" Posho emerged from the rustling refuse sacks with more lemons. "Spare fruit from utility bin bag four. **Oink!** I packed some in case of accidents."

"Brilliant," I cried, beaming as I took hold of the yellow fruits in one hand and tried projecting in the other.

But this time nothing happened. It seemed that Stupendous Man's powers had dried up. I grunted, gritting my teeth, straining to let the lemons' life-energies flow from my fingers. . .

"I say, are you all right, old chap?" Posho looked concerned. "Do you need the lavatory?"

"Yes," I gasped, "but that's not really relevant right now."

It was no good. The lemons were no longer juicing. Merlin's powers, already weakened as we knew, could do no more.

The one-hour-only rule seemed to have gone to pot. How much longer would any of my powers remain?

Then a colossal dragging of flesh against stone

close by signalled the return of the dragon. I glimpsed large, yellowing jaws thrusting down at me. A pool of drool splashed down beside me. . .

And at the smell, my mouth watered hard and I almost laughed out loud in relief.

The dragon's spit smelled like lemon juice! His whole head had taken on the texture and shape of squeezed lemons – even his teeth had turned into rind. He gnashed them uselessly together as he raised one paw, its poisonous razor-claws now a mess of pith and fruit flesh.

I jumped to my heroic feet. "You know what I do with lemons, dragon? I put them in a FRUIT PUNCH!"

And then I clobbered that big, spongy yellow head with a double-fisted **KA-POW!** The blow stung my knuckles, but the effect on the dragon was more dramatic – the great, yellow head jerked aside on the end of its knobbly-bobbly neck in an enormous swing that yanked the bulk of its body skidding across the ground, until. . .

Head made contact with cliff face and –

Never has a sound effect seemed so sweet. The dragon's eyes closed and with a sour roar that sounded more like an iguana gargling with lemon quarters, it went down – and stayed down.

"Wow," I breathed, shaking my aching fists. "I did it! Power Pig, did you see?"

"I saw it, old boy. Wondrous work!" The refined voice came not from the bin bags, but from the misty stretch ahead of me; I could hear him running about. "Though I hope you didn't hit the dragon too hard. We need him alive and angry if the rest of the plan's going to work."

"I don't know my own strength," I admitted, getting up. "And I don't know how much longer I'll have it, either." As I spoke, I remembered Merlin's words on the old parchment:

MY NEMESIS HAS PROMISED THAT SHOULD SHE DETECT AN INTRUDER ATTEMPTING TO INFILTRATE THESE DEFENCES, SHE WILL RETURN SWIFTLY TO DESTROY ME HERSELF. . .

I was already well aware that Viviane knew about me. Was she down below even now, carrying out her evil promise?

The smoke was clearing, and now I could see a pool of blackness in the ground before me, its sinister perimeter surrounded by stone flagstones marked with strange symbols.

"Oi, Posho," I hissed. "I think I've found the dragon's pit."

"Oh?" Posho came racing over, out of breath. "Ah. That would be the hellish pit full of demonic skeleton warriors, hmm? Excellent. Well done."

"Shh!" I whispered. "I can hear something rattling around down there."

Posho swallowed hard. "**Oink!** Probably those skeletons' kneecaps knocking now they know we're coming, eh?"

AH! THE LADY VIVIANE APPROACHES. . .
FOR OUR FINAL MEETING!

"Yeah. Right. Very likely."

"Well, I'll just go and fetch the next lot of utility sacks." With a cheery wave, Posho plunged off into the mist again.

"Good idea," I called. "With my absorbing powers gone, we need to get on with Plan C and just hope we—"

I never got to finish my sentence – a bloodcurdling noise like deranged, jubilant laughter rose from the ground ahead. The hairs on the back of my neck stood up on end.

Harsh, ragged whispers came scraping out from the pit, followed by horrible laughter: "Free. . . we are free again. . . free to kill. . . To slice and dice the souls of our prey. . . To sport their fine flesh upon our warrior bones till it rots around us. . ."

"P-P-P-Power Pig?" I stammered. "Can. . . can you hear those voices. . .?"

"Certainly can, old boy." Posho rejoined me, dragging a clutch of bin bags behind him. "**Oink!** I think those devils are trying to scare us."

I sighed. "If they try any harder I might wet myself."

"Don't worry! I've got these. . ." Posho emptied three large red-and-yellow water-squirting rifles from a bin liner. "Fully charged. And there are spares in these other bags. . ."

"Well, that's great." I shook my head. "Hordes of living skeletons with swords climbing up to get us, but not to worry – we've brought along a stack of water pistols!"

At last I saw them – grasping, bony fingers clawing at the top of the pit. The skeleton warriors began to emerge.

How had I ever convinced myself that risking my life like this was the right thing to do?

As dark sockets in ivory skulls peeped over the edge of the pit, and as bony jaws gibbered and snapped, I wished I could run away. . . like Granddad had, all those years ago.

"Stupendous Man!" Posho turned to me as if he could feel me wobbling, his eyes wide and bright through his beanie hat. "It's all right. We can do this – belief, remember? That's what we need. Belief. . . and a whole load of dirty tricks!"

With every last scrap of courage, I forced a smile. "I hope *clean* tricks will work too. . ."

I tensed myself as the horrific skeletons came climbing out of their foul hidey-hole; five of them… eight. . . ten. . . They swayed about on the flagstones as if acclimatising to their new environment, still giggling, still hissing.

"OK," I said in a wavery voice. "That looks like all of them. Fire on my command. . ."

Slowly, the bony barbarians reached inside their ribcages to draw their swords from the scabbards

stuck to their spines. Then, as if moved in unison by some invisible puppeteer, ten ivory arms raised their weapons high above the grinning skulls...

"All right, Power Pig!" I shouted.

"NOW!"

CHA-CHA-CHA TWENTY-NINE

DANCES WITH SKELETONS

SQUELCH! SQUALCH! SQUILCH! Posho and I squeezed and pumped our plastic weapons, sending clear, gloopy liquid sloshing out at speed, dousing the skeletons and the flagstones they stood on from head to toe. **SPLURT! SPLUSH!** Viviane's warriors glared at us with those ghastly, sightless eyes,

AT AROUND THE SAME TIME,

DOWN BELOW. . .

YOU HAVE BROUGHT HEROES TO SET YOU FREE. I WARNED YOU OF THE CONSEQUENCES!

swords clamped tight in their ivory fingerbones. . .

PLL-SQUERCH! FRRRP-SPLIDDLE! After only a dozen blasts, the shooters were exhausted. The skeletons straightened up, looked at each other. . . then they threw back their skulls and laughed like bony drains.

Posho and I stooped to grab the next of our guns, and started firing again. But the skeletons had had enough. As one, they rushed towards us—

And tripped over, sprawling onto the flagstones, one after another!

BETTER I DIE THAN ENDURE THIS LIVING DEATH!
KADAAM
VERY WELL!

Suddenly, I saw a silver string tied between two large rocks either side of the pit, and I turned to Posho. "You rigged one of your tripwires! That's what you were doing while I KO'ed the dragon!"

"What can I say?" Posho beamed. "I got the most dreadful urge to play a prank – I told you, it's in my nature!"

The skeletons were trying to get back up – but they couldn't. They were too busy slipping and sliding in the gloop we'd used to douse their bones and the ground around them. It was bubbling to a lather now, coating their limbs. They were struggling even to hold their swords.

"I guess you've not come across this stuff before, living in the sixth century," I told the skeletons with a grim smile. "It's just liquid soap and bubble mixture, all mixed up together with a little water." I splattered the skeletons with more of the bubbly slop, and Posho did the same. They writhed helplessly, wailing in a monstrous babble (or bubble) of cries and groans.

"Phew!" Posho wiped piggy sweat from his brow

and straightened his tights. "Time to put Plan J into action?"

I flexed my legs, which still seemed pretty muscled. "OK," I agreed. "Plan J – for **JUMP!**"

So saying, I leaped twenty metres into the air and landed – **K-KRAASH!** – red-grippy-boots-first in the middle of the skeleton pile, grinding ivory hard against soapy flagstones. Again and again I jumped on our foes, careful not to slip, dodging the clumsy swipes of swords and the clutching quiver of fingerbones. And each time I landed I made the impact count. Rib cages snapped, vertebrae crumbled, limbs dislocated.

"Dear, dear," said Posho, wrinkling his snout. "I don't really want to watch this. **Oink!** I'll fetch the next lot of bin bags, shall I?"

"OK," I panted. The skeletons snarled and hissed as I went on jumping up and down, trampling and stamping on their grisly remains, driving out whatever freaky force had animated them.

Finally, the warriors lay broken and scattered in the soapy stew, like the table-leavings of some brutal yet hygiene-obsessed ogre.

With relief I jumped clear – but to my horror, as I did so, Stupendous Man's super-strength seemed to flee my knees. I'd been aiming for the non-slippery ground on the far side of the pit, but my leap was too puny. Instead I found myself scrabbling desperately for the jagged edge of the hideous hell-hole. . .

WHUMP!

I just caught hold of the flagstoned precipice, all but my fingertips dangling down inside the pit. It was dark and dank, stinking and nightmarish, with no bottom in sight.

"Whoa!" I gasped. "So much for my stupendous leg power." I began to pull myself up. "Luckily

my arms are still. . . **oh, NO!**"

My biceps and triceps were deflating like old balloons. I didn't have enough upper body strength to lift myself back up.

"**Posho – Power Pig – quick!**" I yelled. "I'm going to fall! My super powers have gone!"

Weirdly, with that realisation, it wasn't only the thought of falling down into a dark supernatural pit that terrified me. My other horrible thought was: if my stupendousness had suddenly leaked away. . . what did that mean for Merlin?

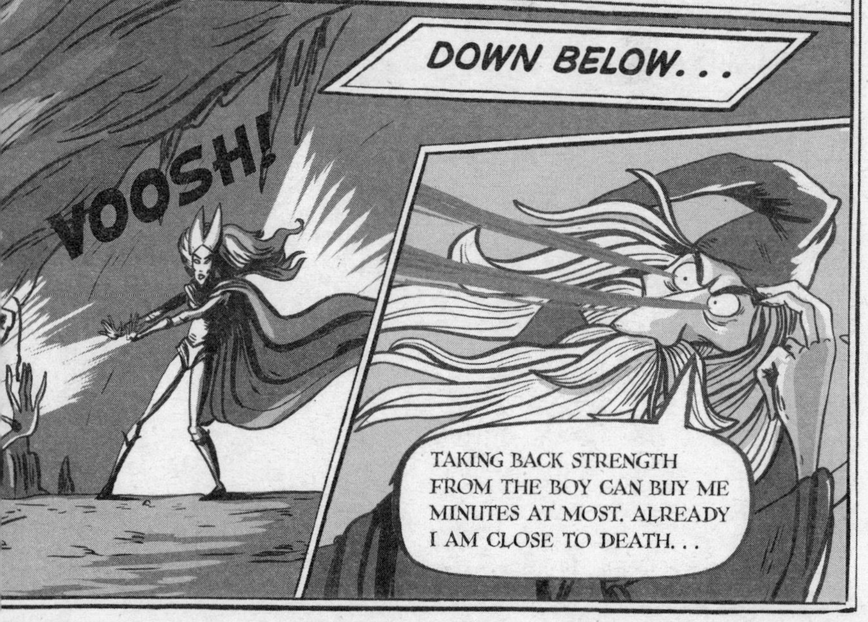

WHILE OUR HEROES STRUGGLE ABOVE,
DOWN BELOW. . .
VOOSH!
TAKING BACK STRENGTH FROM THE BOY CAN BUY ME MINUTES AT MOST. ALREADY I AM CLOSE TO DEATH. . .

"Power Pig!" I shouted again, still clinging on helplessly to the side of the pit. "Posho, please? Where are you?"

"Hang in there, old chap!" Posho came scampering over with another few bin bags. "I'm coming! **Oink!** I'll pull you out! I'll— **WHOOPS!**"

I watched, horror-struck, as Posho skidded in the soapy gloop around the mouth of the pit and went bum-over-trotters into freefall. The bin bags slipped from his grip. . .

Then he dropped like a stone. He only just managed to grab on to my long underwear, snuffling and clinging on for his life. I was glad my pants were on the outside of my costume, or I might have been showing everything by now.

"**Oink!**" He called up. "Sorry, old bean! Bit of a cliffhanger moment, what?"

"I can hardly hold my own weight," I gasped. "With yours too. . ."

No, I told myself, don't give up! You can do this.

Believe! Believe!

I closed my eyes. . . gritted my teeth. . .

But it was no good. My fingers were numb. My arms were full of pins and needles.

With a shout of despair, I finally lost my grip. Next second I was plummeting with Posho into the deathly blackness of the pit. . .

CHAPETR THIRTY

DID IT EVER HURTY!

How far can you fall in a second? I didn't know then and I still don't, but I can tell you it feels like you'll never stop.

I remembered my very favourite Spidey tale (as told in *Amazing Spider-Man* #121-122 from 1973) in which the Green Goblin knocked Spider-Man's girlfriend, Gwen Stacy, from the top of a New York bridge. Spidey tried to save her but he was too late – the force of the fall had already killed her.

The thought didn't exactly comfort me as I plummeted.

Perhaps if poor Gwen had broken her drop as I did – by plunging into a humungous pile of dragon poo – her story would have had a happier (if whiffier) ending.

"OOOOF-URPHHHH!" I spluttered as I splattered

through the stinky stuff. I have no idea what dragons ate in the sixth century and I don't want to know, but at that precise moment I sent a silent thank you to every one of its pre-digested victims for the soft landing.

A jagged circle of white sky hung high above us like a moon, but its light barely reached the dismal depths of the bottom of the pit.

"Ugh!" moaned Posho from somewhere in the mound beside me. "Have you ever heard the expression, 'happy as a pig in poo-poo'? Well, this is one pig who is definitely not amused. **Oink!** This pit is the pits!"

"I guess we should've expected it, Power Pig." I pushed my way out through the spongy, slimy mound. "We knew the dragon was sitting on this pit. Where else was its dung going to go?"

"I'm not surprised those skeletons were keen to get out." Posho hopped down from the muck pile to join me. "Mind you, they looked surprisingly clean once they'd climbed out, didn't they?"

"Shhh," I hissed. "I can hear running water. Which must mean. . ."

"The skeletons took showers before they attacked us?" Posho suggested.

I frowned. "Or that the 'wretchedly evil siren' Merlin talked about is close by. The warning said something about a forbidden door though…"

As I spoke, a ghostly white light flared into life.

FORBIDDEN DOOR

"Just so we don't confuse it with a nice, safe, unforbidden door," said Posho quietly. "**Oink!** How thoughtful. Sounds as though the water is running somewhere behind it."

"Sirens hang out in water," I reminded him. Then, in the glow of the sign, I saw a glimmer of light reflected back by something on the filthy floor – the utility bin bags Posho had dropped down here before falling. I picked them up triumphantly. "Ta-daa!"

Posho came over to check them out. "More good fortune – they had a soft landing too. The stuff inside hasn't even broken!"

"But what's happened to Merlin?" I'd started the trip as a musclebound, powered-up Stupendous Man, and now – judging by the way my smelly costume was hanging off me – I'd gone back to being an ordinary boy.

Helpless. Hopeless.

I remembered Granddad telling me once that you can still be a hero when you're afraid; people who do brave things wouldn't be brave at all if they weren't scared to begin with.

But they were just words. Granddad hadn't been brave, he'd run away. What had I been thinking – that I could redeem all Granddad had lost in his life by sacrificing my own?

Well, I'd made my weird, freaky bed. . . and unfortunately, there was no hiding under it.

"Look!" I said, licking my dry lips. " Little handholds and footholds in the rock. The skeletons must've used them to climb out. But we've got to stay down here and get to Merlin. We've just got to."

"Remarkable." Posho smiled up at me. "It goes to show, heroism isn't just about powers and strength.

Oink! It comes from within, from strength of purpose —"

"— and from the small but vital detail that if Merlin dies, we're stuck here for the rest of our lives," I broke in, before Posho could get too schmaltzy. "Forget Magic, Inc., forget being a famous illustrator. If we ever get out of this, I'll settle for being me. And flip knows, there won't be a whole lot of me left when that dragon I've turned into a lemon-saurus wakes up and comes sniffing around for revenge."

"It can't claw and poison us anymore," said Posho brightly. "And it won't find it as easy to eat us."

"Really? We're in the bottom of its toilet pit! Who's got the advantage?" I reminded him – as an ominous dragon roar sounded from high above us. "I reckon this is gonna become a very unhealthy place to be any moment now."

"Then we've got nothing much to lose by going through the forbidden door," said Posho. Cautiously, he tried the handle. "Locked! How can we get in?"

"Hmm. . ." I spotted something dull white by the

door and scooped it up from the ground. "Would you believe a skeleton key?" It was a fingerbone, covered in soapy mixture; must've fallen during my earlier trampling spree. I slipped it into the lock, and sure enough, it turned. The door opened at once and spilled sea-green light over us. . .

And then a siren began to wail. Not the devious, dangerous woman-wraith type siren, but something like a police siren. I jammed my mucky hands over my ears, and Posho pulled his hat down even further over his head as we pushed inside.

We found ourselves in a green-lit cave, its ceiling spiked with stalactites, a large pool of water with a cascading fountain in its centre. On the other side of the cave was an enormous round boulder – the last thing that stood between Posho and me and Merlin's prison. From the looks of things, just as we'd feared, even Stupendous Man would've struggled to shift it.

I looked around for the source of the wailing noise. It seemed to be coming from a small candle spinning round in a holder in the wall.

"Oink!" Posho frowned. "This isn't the siren I expected."

Suddenly the noise cut off – as a hefty, pale-green woman clothed in seaweed and shells burst up from the pool. **"Oooh!"** she boomed, shaking her spiky blonde hair. "I was just having a good dream! About fish. I was catching hundreds of fish and arranging them in order of size and width of their dorsal fins. It was dead good. . . Why'd you have to wake me up. Eh? Eh?"

I spoke to Posho from the corner of my mouth. "This isn't the siren I expected either."

"We didn't wake you, madam," said Posho smoothly. "That siren was responsible."

"I'm the siren," she snapped.

"No, I mean the noisy thing," I tried.

The siren looked affronted. "Noisy? A lovely singer like me? What a cheek!"

"No, I mean the other siren!" I pointed to the spinning candle. "*That* siren."

"Fat siren? Who are you calling a fat siren?" The watery woman put her clawed hands on her big green hips. "You come crashing in here, calling me names, wanting a bath like those silly skeletons I suppose, and then you—"

"We'll skip the bath, thanks, we're kind of in a hurry," I said – as a huge, bone-shaking roar from up above reminded me that the lemony dragon could come hunting down here at any moment. That was good as far as our masterplan went, but bad in just about every other way possible. We had to be ready!

"So. . ." I gave the siren my most winning smile. "D'you think you could let us pass?"

"That would be splendid." Posho beamed too. "See, we really need to reach the Big Man tucked away behind the even bigger stone there, and—"

"What?" The siren scowled. "No one gets in there. Especially not dirty troublemakers like you who don't even want a bath." A nasty smile hooked at her features. "I think it's time I sang you my song of doom! How sweet and sad it is. . . How quickly you will fall under my spell – and under my water. How quickly you will forget that trying to breathe in that water is a foolish thing to do. How—"

"—long before you shut up," I cried, pulling a portable, battery-operated CD player from the bin bag. As the siren opened her mouth to protest – or possibly to sing, how should I know – I pressed play, and track one from *Best Dubstep Anthems In the House, Volume Seven* began blaring at top volume. Not my own personal choice of music, but the first CD we'd grabbed from Harvest Boy's hole in the ground.

The siren's eyes widened in outrage and she started shouting at us to switch it off.

"Sorry," I yelled, "can't hear you!" And with a wink at Posho, I ran over to the boulder with the other bin bag in my hand, trying not to trip over in my now-oversized boots.

Posho examined the gigantic rock. "**Oink!** It really *is* limestone. We're in luck."

"Course we are," I yelled over the boom and thud of the beatbox. "We're being deafened by dance music in the underground cave of an angry overweight siren in the bottom of a dung chute with a killer dragon-monster due to burst in any moment—"

I was drowned out – even J-Lo and Pitbull were drowned out – by a terrifying roar. The dragon was close – peering down into the pit, its yellow, bestial head brushing against the forbidden doorway.

"Company!" I quivered, flattening myself against the boulder. "Right. Good. Perfect."

"Now you're for it!" shrieked the siren, splashing her tail happily in the water.

"Of course!" Posho cried. "That first siren wasn't

only the real siren's wake-up call – **Oink!** – it was a signal to the other guardians that the Big Man's prison had almost been breached, to bring them running back here in case they'd been lured somewhere else."

"Or stamped into bits by a superhero," I added. With trembling hands I reached into the last bin bag, pulled out a large bottle of malt vinegar and emptied it all over the limestone.

See, I learned in school once that the acetic acid in the vinegar dissolves the calcium carbonate in limestone. . .

However, my assault on the stone did nothing but make it smell like chips. The siren laughed. The dragon roared and began to squeeze its lemony head inside the cave.

"Yes, O Guardian of the Pit!" howled the siren. "Come! Destroy the intruders!"

"Power Pig," I shouted. "The plan was that Stupendous Man would absorb the vinegar-power and stream it into the boulder—"

"So that a well-targeted trotter could crack the limestone like an egg," Posho agreed. "Hmm,

I wonder. . ." He weighed up his own bottle – and suddenly chucked it at the siren! It cracked her right on the forehead, and with an off-key hoot of anger, she fell back into the water – and stayed there.

"**Oink!**" Posho squealed with delight. "The vinegar's useless, but the bottle was well worth bringing along!"

"Nice throw, Power Pig." I hugged him and gladly switched off the music. But with no competing soundtrack, the dragon's growls seemed louder, deeper, even scarier.

Posho gulped. "Let's hope that Plan DD will add more power to our chemical plans!"

Plan DD stood for 'Dragon Drool'. Anticipating that Merlin's powers might be on the wane by the time we breached the siren's cave, we'd decided to make the dragon lemony so that its spit became citric acid – like the vinegar, another good dissolver of limestone.

That's why I didn't turn the dragon into bin bags or plastic or something! They would be lousy for breaking big rocks.

Now we could only hope that the citric element was somehow amplified by the dragon's gigantic size and nastiness, because if it wasn't. . .

Finally, the dragon succeeded in forcing its head inside. It roared with renewed anger at the sight of the socked-out siren, then spat a fierce, sticky stream of super-concentrated lemon juice right at us.

I dived aside but – "**UGHHH!**" I spluttered and spat as a few stray splashes caught my face – and burned there like fire. I floundered forward and threw myself into the siren's pool, desperately trying to wash the stuff off.

But Posho was proving a harder target. I'd seen him bounce nimbly around the attic before, but now, crouched in the pool for cover, I watched him leap and somersault back and forward in front of the boulder, drawing the dragon's fire – or rather, its lemon juice.

The dragon spat and wheezed and yowled. Its neck had to be at full-stretch, it couldn't squeeze any more of itself inside. That fact seemed to be making it more and more frustrated.

"Come on, old chap, splash me if you can!" Power

Pig was maintaining positively Spider-Mannish levels of off-putting banter with his foe. "**Oink!** Most pigs prefer an apple stuffed in their mouths before serving, but I like something with a little more bite – **Oink!** – which is not to draw attention to your poor squashy lemon-rind teeth, but really – they are rubbish, aren't they?"

Again and again the dragon spat sizzling citric acid at the limestone as it tried to hit Posho. The boulder smoked. Plan DD might just work, I thought excitedly. We might just be able to break through the boulder and force our way inside. . .

But then – "**Aieeeeeeee!**" – Posho's luck finally ran out (or the dragon's luck finally ran in, depending on where you were standing) and he took a citric blast right to the chest. It broke over him like a fruity tsunami and smashed him back against the boulder, mask askew and leotard steaming.

"Power Pig!" I yelled helplessly. "Are you all right? Get up! Please!"

But that bravest of pigs lay prone, and still.

"Forget your little swine of a friend," came a

fishwife shout in my ear. "Worry about yourself!"

I spun round to find the siren had recovered, raising a restraining hand to the dragon to calm its lemon-fuelled frenzy. As the beast bowed its head and stopped growling at her command, she smiled at me nastily; there was a lump on her head and she looked ready to dish out a few of her own.

"Now, my little troublemaker," she hissed, "I shall sing you such a song. . . a melody so exquisitely deadly, it could charm even the strongest soul into a deep but deathless sleep. . . A sleep from which you will never awake!"

Terrified, I tried to splash out of the pool – but water was the siren's element. She swam up to me in a second and caught hold of my wrist.

Then she started to sing – notes of deep and terrible beauty. They echoed radiantly through my head, stunning all other senses, suppressing all needs other than the need to listen on. . . to succumb. . . to sleep and never to wake again. How could I resist? No one could possibly resist, the siren had said so. . .

Dimly, I heard another noise – lower, louder, more

violent, shaking the air to smoke and dust around me…

And then the dragon reared up and roared and the siren's song became a squeal of alarm as—

Brr-ka-TOOOOOM!

That astonishing sound effect was the last thing I heard before my head exploded. Not literally – that would be messy. I mean exploded with pain, as something struck me on the temple with enough force to knock me clear out of the pool.

I landed on my back with a thump and a gasp, ears ringing and vision blurred. But even so I guessed quickly what had hit me.

There were little lumps of limestone scattered all around.

Stunned, I looked up. The boulder blocking Merlin's cave had blown apart. The way was clear, and dark and gaping.

Instinctively, I looked over at the dragon – why had it stopped growling? Answer: it was wearing chunks of limestone as a fetching face-mask. They had thumped and pounded into his lemony flesh and left him well and truly out of the game.

Exit the dragon.

But the siren stood unharmed in the pool – and now recovered her voice. "So!" she snarled. "The final barrier to Merlin's prison is undone! But the Big Man shall never escape." She took a deep breath. "Time for my closing number!"

Once again, she began to sing, more eerily and awfully than ever. I clasped my hands over my ears…

But found there was no need. My poor lugholes

were ringing so loudly I couldn't hear the deadly details of her tune. I could resist her power. Result!

Still in shock, my head killing me and every sense petrified, I lay still, pretending I was hypnotised – and half-wishing that I really was – as an echoing voice rang out from the darkness in the cave:

"Stop! Stop singing. . . Stop!"

"Ha! Now the stone is gone, you can hear me, wizard – and you too shall sleep the sleep eternal!" The siren raised her voice, belting out her song at the top of her watery lungs, every syllable dripping with evil. "Never more shall you know the world about you! Never more shall you awaken! Never—***Eeeeeep!***"

The siren's voice caught in her throat like a fishbone, and her eyes bulged at the sight of the figure striding out of the cave and into the light. . .

Were my shattered senses deceiving me? This didn't look like Merlin. Not unless being locked up all that time had really changed the Big Man. No, this was a woman, thin and pale, her cruel face framed by lank red hair, her eyes wild like a winter sea.

It had to be. . . it could only be. . .

"B-b-b-boss?" The siren did her impression of a fish yanked out of water, and it was good – hands flapping, eyes bulging, mouth jerking open and shut.

I knew how she felt.

Viviane!

Here! Now!

She took a slow step closer. . . and another. . .

If I thought I'd been scared before, the fear I felt in that moment went right off the scale. She's gonna kill me, I thought helplessly. She's gonna destroy me. . . She's gonna turn me to dust.

"You. . . fool. . .!" Viviane's cold blue eyes narrowed. "Now— I can't— get your song— out of— my HEAD. . ."

"Boss!" Looking terrified, the siren had turned a sickly shade of yellow. "I'm so sorry! Speak to me, boss! Please!"

It was no good. Viviane's mouth had closed as heavily as her eyes. Her fingers twitched, clutching at thin air. Slowly, as if her limbs were turning to jelly, she slipped to the ground. Just as slowly, the evidence of my eyes penetrated my daze and the facts fixed themselves onto my disbelieving senses. It wasn't Merlin who'd been bewitched by the siren's song, I realised with a rush of giddy excitement.

It was Viviane herself!

"La-la-la-la," came a discordant boom from the cave. A stooped, broad-shouldered man came shambling out in a shabby smock, his bony fingers stuck in his ears, chanting just as he'd done in the supermarket a few days back – or rather, fifteen hundred years in the future.

The din in my ears seemed to fade a little and strength crept back into my body. "Merlin!" I breathed. "You're alive!"

He couldn't hear me of course. "La-li-la-la— oh, hello, there!" He smiled at the siren, who by now seemed utterly speechless with shock. "Have you stopped that racket now? No offence, my dear, but I couldn't hear a note. I was too busy chanting with my fingers in my ears." He looked down at the prone female figure by his feet. "I must thank you for putting Viviane into a deathless sleep – I honestly wasn't sure how on earth I was going to beat her!"

"Don't gloat yet, old man!" snarled the siren, finally finding her voice. "I'll make you hear my song and then— **OOF!**" She screeched as another rock hurtled out of nowhere and whacked her right on the head. "Ow! Not. . . again. . ."

SPLOSH! The siren flopped forwards on her face

and sank to the bottom of her pool, snoring bubbles as she went.

"Arthur's bodkins!" Merlin exclaimed, looking about. "Who conked her on the head—?"

"ME! **Oink-oink-oink!** For the second time today!" With a thrill I saw that Posho was back on his trotters. His tights were baggy and wrinkled, his leotard soaked and his cape askew. . .

And yet as he stood there – a proud smile hanging beneath his moustache – I had never seen him look more heroic.

"Big Man. . . my most honoured Merlin. . . I am the peerless Power Pig." Posho scampered over to me and gently helped me to my feet. "And this quite remarkable young fellow who has risked all to help you, is the one and only Stupendous Man."

"Er. . . hi," I murmured, plucking gingerly at my soaked and ill-fitting costume.

Merlin looked us up and down, doubtful at first – but then with a smile to warm those craggy features. "Stewart Penders. . . Descendant of Garry Penders. . . Titanic True Believer in the power of comics. . ."

"Glad you're OK," I said groggily. "How did you get out?"

"With the last of my power I deflected Viviane's magical attack towards the limestone boulder. . ." Merlin's eyes were like lanterns in the dim light. "Of course, had you not so ably weakened the rock with acid, it would never have burst apart like that. Truly. . . I owe the two of you my life."

Posho oinked quietly. "I would never have lived at all if not for you, Merlin. I know I have been a terrible burden to you in your imprisonment."

"I fear my unkindness to you has been a burden worse by far, pig." He paused and smiled again. "Power Pig, I should say. Well! Know that this day you have proved to me my magic was not misspent. And know too that I consider you both to be true superheroes – yea, of the highest and most dazzling rank!"

I felt a dizzying rush of elation. . . followed by just plain dizziness. Merlin hobbled over and placed a warm hand on my shoulder, as if to hold me up.

"Uh, I'm really stoked that this worked out well," I said quickly. "It so nearly didn't."

"Yes, Viviane revealed her trick with the magic ink brush to me, while she was trying to kill me, back there in the cave. I should have realised, a tool for good can always be turned into a tool for evil." Merlin smiled and nodded thoughtfully. "And yet, I feel a greater good can still come of this. . ."

"That's cool. I'm happy. Really." My head throbbed harder and without Merlin's hand to hold me up my legs began to buckle. "Uh, guys? I know that superheroes aren't supposed to faint, but—"

You can guess what happened next, right?

CLONK!

Everything went black.

CHAPTER THIRTY-WON

WHAT PRICE VICTORY?

I woke up in my bed. Back in Granddad's house. It had all been a dream.

THE END

NOOOOOOOOOOOOO!!!

Not really.

But I did wake up in my bed, back in Granddad's house. In my pyjamas and everything. And with a head clouded with weirdness and worry. It was three o'clock in the morning and I had no idea what was going on. Until I noticed a comic lay open on my chest. A comic made from old parchment.

A Magic, Inc. comic.

I snatched it up and turned to the first page. . .

EPILOGUE
... or is it the PROLOGUE?
WILL STEW BE ALL RIGHT?
A LITTLE MAGIC HEALS ALL WOUNDS.
I OWE YOU SUPERHEROES MUCH.
AND WHILE MY WORLD MAY NOT BE READY FOR COMICS, MY WORK WILL GO ON - IN YOUR WORLD!

I turned the page – but the rest of the mag was blank. So I looked at the front cover. . .

And there was Stupendous Man, looking cool and ready for action, beneath a cool-looking logo in a language I didn't need to translate:

THE NEW ADVENTURES OF

STUPENDOUS MAN

Script by Stewart Penders. Drawn by Stewart Penders.

Inked by Stewart Penders. Lettered by Stewart Penders.

A Magic, Inc. Production (Magic, Inc. owned by **STEWART PENDERS**)

"My own comic," I breathed. "My own comics company. . ."

A tingling thrill went through me. On the bedside table I saw a brush, and a dark bottle beside it.

A bottle of magic ink. Full to the brim. It was darkest blue, the colour of wild oceans. The colour of the sky outside.

As I looked through the window in a daze at the twinkling stars, the view was suddenly blocked by a short, familiar figure.

"Posho!" I almost yelled it out in delight as I opened the window catch. "Posho, come inside!"

"Thank you, old chap, I will. **Oink!**" The pig entered with a flourish and I hugged him tight. "But I've told you before, when I'm in costume the name's not Posho – it's Power Pig!"

And, as I took him in properly, to my amazement, I couldn't think of a better name to describe him. Gone was the rubbishy old homemade outfit, the little girl leotards and middle-aged lady tights. He was wearing a cool, all-in-one lycra number in mauve and purple, with thick gauntlets and a dynamic PP on his chest.

I grinned. "So. . . Merlin gave you this gear for your part in his rescue?"

"He did." Posho preened himself. "Rather splendid, don't you think?"

"Not bad." I nodded approvingly. "So, what special powers did you get with it?"

"None that I didn't have already," said Posho proudly. "And now that I've got a taste for daring rescues, I'm off to perform some more of them – wherever my trotters take me."

"Ah. . ." A little wetness stung the backs of my eyes. "You're leaving, then?"

"I've stayed in this house for twenty years. **Oink!** I think it's time I moved on, don't you?" Posho smiled up at me. "Thank you, old bean. If you hadn't believed in me, I could have been stuck here for ever."

"You believed in me too. And in Stupendous Man." I smiled back. "Made a pretty good team, didn't we?"

Posho nodded proudly, and pointed to the ink and brush on the table. "And now you're the boss of Magic, Inc., old boy, you'll be hatching all sorts of far-fetched exploits – from the safety of your own home." He pointed to a small, fold-away drawing board that had appeared in the corner of my bedroom. "That looks like a good place to get started. The Big Man said it was fully charged with artistic vibes from some of the top names in comics. . ."

I rubbed my eyes in amazement – but the drawing board stayed solid and real. "Been a busy boy, that Merlin, hasn't he?" I murmured, with a smile.

"He's got all the time and freedom in the world, now," said Posho. "Thanks to us." The pig crossed to the window, then looked back and gave a sort of bashful salute. "Pip, pip, old chap. I shall miss you."

"Then learn to aim straight," I muttered, "you're a superhero now." I grabbed him close in a final farewell hug. "Come back and visit sometime – promise?"

"Naturally!" Posho winked. "I wonder how high up you'll be in the world of comics by then?"

"Mmm. I wonder that too." I turned and gazed at the magic ink. Such a powerful tool. Such an incredible prize.

But after the risks I'd taken to earn it, to draw

perfectly every time felt somehow. . . safe. I didn't know if I wanted to let that brush and ink do all the work for me. Not any more.

"What do you think, Power Pig?" I began, turning towards him. "Do you think I should . . .?"

But I saw only curtains catching in the breeze from the open window. Posho was already seeking answers to his own questions in the best possible way – by running out into the night and taking chances as they came. By living life to the fullest.

"Bye for now, Posho," I called softly.

"STEW!" Mum complained from the bedroom next door. "Will you stop mumbling and go to sleep?"

"It's half-three in the morning," Dad added.

"Is it time to get up?" Lib speculated – to two resounding grown-up 'NO!'s.

"It's time to sleep on things," I decided, plumping up my pillow.

There was no need for quick decisions. I'd suss it out in time. Just like I'd suss out my new school, new friends, new clubs and all the rest. It would all fall into place. I'd make sure of it.

My secret identity is Stewart Penders.

I'M STUPENDOUS, MAN.

M
INK

ACKNOWLEDGMENTS

Massive thanks go to everyone who has worked so hard on making *Magic Ink* into the book you now hold in your hands, but especially the following:

To Venetia Gosling and Ingrid Selberg for wanting me to write for them.

To Jane Buckley for tireless perfectionism on the look of the book.

To Emma Young, for peerless editing.

To Jim Field, who not only coped with my demands for multiple illustration personalities but who made it look effortless.

To Philippa Milnes-Smith, my agent, for all she does.

Thanks also to Anthony Holbourn for Latin translation!

And, of course, to Stan Lee, Jack Kirby, Steve Ditko, John Romita Jr, Roy Thomas and so many others, whose superheroes and villains captured a small boy's imagination and never let it go.

STEVE COLE

Steve Cole spent a happy childhood dreaming of being a superhero and being silly and loud whenever he wasn't sleeping. At school his teachers often despaired of him - one of them went so far as to ban him from her English lessons, which enhanced his reputation no end.

Having grown up liking stories, he went to university to read more of them before working as an editor of books and magazines for both children and grown-ups (including his childhood favourite, *Doctor Who*). He wrote books in his spare time until 2002 when he decided to make his living as a writer. Since then he has created several successful book series including *Astrosaurs, Cows In Action, The Slime Squad, Thieves Like Us* and *Z. Rex*.

He lives in Buckinghamshire with his family, and still secretly hopes to be bitten by something radioactive that will give him superpowers.

STEVE COLE

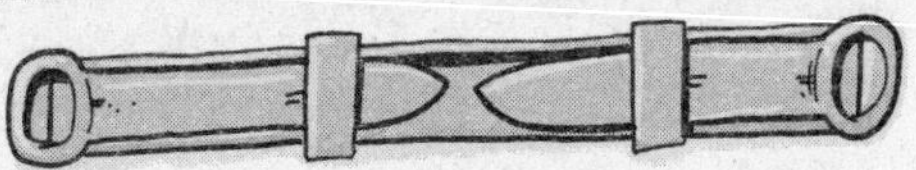

JIM FIELD

JIM FIELD

Jim grew up in Farnborough and drew from a very early age (just like Stew) with a burning ambition to 'make cartoons', possibly due to Tony Hart and *Rolf's Cartoon Time*, which were on telly at the time. In his early teens he was a big fan of Marvel comics and made his own superhero series of comics called *Extres*.

He studied animation at Hull School of Art and Design, graduating in 2002, before starting work in the animation industry as a director for Partizan in London. Meanwhile, he was also penning his way as a freelance illustrator. Jim illustrated the two-book series *Quentin Quirk's Magic Works*, written by Kelly McKain, and his first picture book, *Cats Ahoy!*, written by Peter Bently, won the Booktrust Roald Dahl Funny Prize in 2011 and was nominated for the Kate Greenaway award. Since then Jim has worked on several more picture books, and umpteen fiction books.
He lives in London with his three bikes and three guitars, and is happiest when he's drawing.

Coming in 2014. . .

ALIENS STINK!

by Steve Cole

Some seriously **weird** stuff is happening on **Planet Earth.**

Pollution is cleaned up overnight. A sweet smell fills the air. Strange lights are seen in the skies. . . Could they possibly be **UFOs?** Have aliens come to fix our world?

Only one boy and his dad – and possibly his goldfish – know that the truth is **stranger, scarier** – and a whole lot **smellier. . .**

But what the hecking flip are they going to do about it?

Turn over for a sneaky peek at the first chapter . . .

CHAPTER ZERO

I'm writing this on a plane.

Not, like, a holiday plane. It's a private plane, big and flashy. Destination unknown, but I'm guessing it's somewhere remote. There's nothing but snow to look at through the window, only I can't look 'cos it's blinding bright in the sunshine.

I don't know who owns this plane. I don't know who's flying it. I don't know who the guys are in the seats beside me or even what country they come from.

I certainly don't know what kind of guns they're carrying. They're chunky and big. The guns, I mean.

And the guys too, come to think of it.

All of which is freaking me out just a little.

I'm hoping my fish, Herbert, is OK. He's locked away in the luggage hold. . . in his bowl, obviously. What if his water spills everywhere – or starts to freeze? What if his bowl cracks?

In the seat opposite, Dad's freaking out too, I can tell – though he's trying not to show it.

It's not just the fact we've been forced onto this flight going who-knows-where. Dad thinks flying is evil at the best of times: noise pollution, air pollution, greenhouse gases... For him, the flight must be passing like a giant, petrified poo – slow and painful, with one hell of a stink brewing.

Where will we end up? No one's saying. Squinting outside, there's still only snow.

A plate of cold pizza sits in front of me. It's the only food on board, they say. Dad won't touch it 'cos it's got meat on it. Pepperoni. Actual PEPPERONI.

If I picked up a slice I could taste meat for the first time in my life. . . But I'm so scared, I can't eat a thing.

A part of me thinks, what a waste of a perfect

opportunity! A bigger part of me thinks, how can you even be thinking about your stomach at a time like this? A slightly smaller part of me thinks, how can you even be thinking about how you can be thinking about your stomach at a time like this?

Everyone knows that some seriously freaky stuff's been going on in the world lately – unless you've been asleep or locked up or meditating in a cave for the last few months. And if you have, then LUCKY YOU. Ignorance is bliss, right?

Well, ignorance is also dangerous.

If Planet Earth's in as much doo-doo as I think it is, someone needs to find us a new planet to rent.

And meantime, 'cos I'm closer to the action than you are – the real, top secret action – I can give you the lowdown on what's really going on. It'll help me to distract myself. 'Cos. . . remember what I told you about there being nothing to see through the window but snow and sun-glare?

That just changed.

And what I'm looking at now, you would not believe.

So while Dad and everyone else on board are shouting and swearing and the guys with guns are jumping around in the aisle like someone weed on their shoes, putting my story down in words will at least give me something to do for the next little while.

'Cos – WHOA!!! – no way am I ever looking out of this plane window again. . .

BRAND NEW!
VISIT THE MAGIC INK PRODUCTIONS
WEBSITE FOR MORE MAGIC FUN:
WWW.MAGICINKPRODUCTIONS.COM
Find out even more
about the characters
in the Magic Ink world
Get a sneak peek at
forthcoming books from
Steve Cole
HELP